I0744969

Iris ♥

CHRIS KENISTON

Indie House Publishing

Indie House Publishing

BOOKS BY CHRIS KENISTON

Hart Land
Heather
Lily
Violet
Iris
Hyacinth

Farraday Country
Adam
Brooks
Connor
Declan
Ethan
Finn
Grace
Hannah
Ian
Jamison
Keeping Eileen

Aloha Series Heartwarming Edition
Aloha Texas
Almost Paradise
Mai Tai Marriage
Dive Into You
Look of Love
Love by Design
Love Walks In
Flirting with Paradise

Surf's Up Flirts
(Aloha Series Companions)
Shall We Dance
Love on Tap
Head Over Heels
Perfect Match
Just One Kiss
It Had to Be You

**Other Books
By Chris Keniston**

Honeymoon Series
Honeymoon for One
Honeymoon for Three

Family Secrets Novels
Champagne Sisterhood
The Homecoming
Hope's Corner

Original Aloha Series
Waikiki Wedding

ACKNOWLEDGEMENTS

Writing this series has been a fun adventure for me. I hope learning about each wonderful member of the Hart family has been as much fun for you as it has for me!

In the case of *Iris*, I have to thank my daughter and her friend Allie for years ago braving the shores of Thailand and playing with elephants. Thankfully the experience was a happy one, but spawned the opening paragraphs none the less.

One of the challenges for authors is coming up with interesting careers and situations. Some come easily and some not so much. For our hero I have the very talented fantasy author Regina Richards to thank. Who knows what Eric would have done for a living if she'd not helped brainstorm this story!

Once again I need to tip my hat to my Aunt Mary for another delicious recipe! I hope at least some of you are trying these out.

Time to sit back and enjoy Iris while I work away on the next book!

Thanks for reading!

CHAPTER ONE

Elephants are majestic animals. A long list of adjectives popped into Iris Colby's head. Huge being at the top, followed by enormous—no, make that ginormous. Next would be powerful, and as the animal in question lifted his trunk up high in the air blowing out a deafening sound that bore an unbearable resemblance to an off-key tuba, the word petrifying beat out all the others.

"Iris," a voice called from the thatched greenery behind her.

She really hadn't wanted to accompany the Throckmortons to India. Her parents had told her dreadful things about the weather, the crowds, the food, and assorted unpleasantries. On the other hand, romantic childhood images of the Taj Mahal and devoted princes urged her to be more adventurous. Get out of her comfort zone. Away from the big cities. Anyone could shop the Champs-Élysées in Paris, but to ride an elephant in India?

The elephant stomped closer, shaking the ground beneath her feet at the same time the voice called a little louder. It was the touch of the giant beast's trunk on her shoulder that had her voice tearing from deep in her lungs.

"Miss Iris," another voice screeched almost as loudly.

It took Iris a few seconds to realize she was no longer in India, or Thailand, or Timbuktu for that matter. She no longer worked for the

Throckmortons, and the poor woman she'd just scared half to death was the Belton's new housekeeper. "Sorry."

Now halfway across the room, standing frozen in place like a petrified tree trunk, the shaken woman managed to exhale a barely controlled breath. "You said not to let you nap more than an hour."

Iris glanced at the clock on her nightstand. Yes. Sleeping had been difficult. Ever since her run in with that all too playful elephant on the last trip, her nights had been restless and filled with worst case scenarios. Not even changing jobs, taking the prospect of distant travel and spoiled full-blown teenagers off the table, had helped. "Thank you, Ella. I'll be downstairs momentarily."

"Also, Master Michael phoned. He's been invited to dinner at the Carmichael's. What shall I tell him?"

Running the list of acceptable companions and invitations the Beltons had left her, she clearly remembered the Carmichaels were at the top of the yes-by-all-means list. "That will be fine."

Wringing her hands, Iris shook her head and blew out a sigh. The Belton's daughter Tiffany would be home soon. Then the battles would ensue. Homework first, girl talk second. More than once Iris had come close to burning the pre-teen's cell phone in effigy to whoever had actually invented the blasted thing. The privileged daughter had been helicoptered her entire life. Who was Iris kidding, the girl was just plain spoiled rotten, and Iris doubted any amount of restricted parenting at this point could turn that around. Tiffany would no doubt become one of those uppity society mothers more than ready to raise another generation of self-absorbed children who would grow up to believe everything in life could be resolved with a signature at the bottom of a check. Any delusions Iris may have had that she could make a difference in these pre-teens lives had pretty much come and gone as swiftly as her nightmares.

"Would you like a cup of tea?"

Lost in her own thoughts, Iris hadn't even noticed Ella had remained watching her. The fear in the housekeeper's voice had shifted to concern in her eyes. More than one night, Ella had come into the kitchen when she should have been sleeping because she'd heard Iris making tea. "That would be nice, thank you."

Her cell phone beeped and the familiar number brought a smile to her face. "Hello, General."

"You still sound…tired."

Her grandfather was the most imposing man she knew, and yet she loved him with all her heart. "Have I said thank you lately?"

"Thank you?" The gruff voice faltered in confusion.

"For raising Mom and my aunts like normal people and making sure all of us kids did normal things and grew up level headed and well—"

"Normal," he repeated. "Yes, you have. But I can't take the credit for that. If your grandmother had let me have my way, you'd all have grown up with revelry, mess call, and lights out. Could have been like boot camp." The last part came out sort of wistful and made Iris smile.

The man had indeed tried to impose early to bed and early to rise rules on his granddaughters and every so often even on his guests, but their Grams had indeed kept things blissfully unmilitary. "Then thank you for marrying Grams."

The bluster in the old man's voice made her laugh out right. She wasn't sure she'd ever heard the man be in anything except utter and complete control.

"Yes. Well. About you coming to the lake," he sputtered.

How could she have forgotten? Working as a nanny for New York's upper crust, she'd done her share of traveling. The Throckmortons, however, had upped the concept of travel a notch. The family had her traipsing around every nook and cranny of the world while homeschooling their two children. Not that they ever really had a home, more a house for the season. She hadn't minded at first, but as the cute children sprouted into disrespectful self absorbed teenagers, the job had grown tiresome. India was the last straw. Not to mention, despite her best efforts, those same cell phone addicted teens had developed an attitude of entitlement where they'd begun to look down at her as mere hired help. That made Iris laugh. She could match her education and pedigree notch for notch with the best families on the New York social register, she just didn't see any reason to. Working for the Beltons was supposed to be more of a nine to five, Monday through Friday arrangement, allowing her more time to visit her family on the lake. She missed spending time with her cousins. Their lives were moving on and she was beginning to feel a bit left out. In the weeks she'd been at the Briarcliff estate, the children had been left solely in her care more often than not. There could be no taking even an afternoon off, never mind escape for a weekend to the lake. Like it or not, she was seriously over being responsible for other people's children. "Things aren't working out the way I'd hoped."

"Young lady, you were very clear. This latest governess job would be strictly weekdays only."

She stifled a giggle. No one used the word governess anymore. "As I said, things haven't worked out as planned. Mr. Belton has had to extend his business dealings in London and Mrs. Belton has seen fit to join him."

"Perhaps if they didn't have someone as competent as you to rely on, the mother would return to her post and do her duty."

Yes, Iris would get right on explaining to Abigail Smythe Belton how she needed to come home and do her duty. Iris glanced out the window. Although. "You know, sir, that may not be a bad idea at all."

Now all she had to do was enlighten her newest employer that the General always knew best.

• • • •

This was the right decision. The right thing to do. Definitely the right thing. Glancing at the rearview mirror at the two young children in the back seat, Eric Johnson prayed this was the right thing to do. If it weren't, he was just plain out of ideas.

The moping four year old little boy clutched at the stuffed leopard backpack and shifted his gaze from the window to the front seat. "Are we here yet?"

"Almost."

Hart House couldn't be close enough. The same question had been asked and answered multiple times in the last thirty minutes. Just ahead, to the side of the road, a huge sign with a lake vista background covered in large neon white letters declared Welcome to Lawford. The vise that had been squeezing his heart for the last few hours, a painful reminder this was his last hope, eased slightly.

According to the GPS, the rambling white house, literally pretty as a picture, should be just around the bend. His only connection to the past and the future had been the cheery card he'd come across confirming the reservation for another perfect family getaway.

Perched deep into the wooded lot, the rambling Victorian house boasted a wrap around front porch that invited a weary traveler to sit down, take a load off his feet, and indulge in a cool beverage, almost whispering you made the right choice. Nothing could have made a prettier sight. Well, maybe Adele waving madly with a bright smile across her face.

The circle drive seemed to cut the property in sections. Elevated on a slight hill sat the welcoming house. Opposite the drive, patches of green grass dotted with small white cabins cascaded down the hillside to the lake. Any other time and he would have simply taken in the splendid view. The postcard hadn't exaggerated.

"I want to go home." The little boy frowned, strangling his stuffed backpack. His only comfort.

As expected, the stubborn cry had wakened his sleeping sister. Almost two years older, Emily blinked quickly, looked left then right, and for a split-second Eric thought he saw a spark of contentment in her eyes before she silently turned to her brother and softly whispered, "Me too."

"You're here!" The loud, enthusiastic call startled Eric away from the sad sight in the rearview mirror.

"We've been waiting." A grinning middle-aged woman in a gingham dress reminiscent of something Andy Taylor's aunt would have worn, clapped her hands together. "My, how you've grown."

Beside the friendly greeter trotting in their direction, a sleek woman with shoulder length gray hair practically glided down the stairs and flashed a photo perfect smile. "Oh, my Lucy, I think you're right." Even wearing a bright blue and orange flowing floor length dress, she reminded him of royalty. Her face could have easily been the inspiration for a hundred ancient statues.

The first woman, Lucy, swung the rear door open before he could fully escape from the car. She looked to Emily. "I have peanut butter cookies fresh out of the oven."

This time he was sure a flash of delight flickered in his niece's eyes. He'd have to make a note. Emily liked peanut butter cookies.

"And you, young Mr. Gavin," she turned, smiling at the frowning boy, "chocolate chip with M&Ms for you."

The frown slipped and a smile most definitely pursed the child's lips for a full five seconds before he remembered he wanted to go home.

"Come on now," the woman clapped her hands, "can't let the cookies get cold."

Though still not smiling, neither child complained. To Eric's surprise, they'd unbuckled their safety belts, scrambled out of the car and each taking hold of a proffered hand, followed the woman up the stairs. The almost too-friendly woman continued talking as though this was the happiest day in anyone's life, including the two silent children.

"It takes time."

He'd forgotten about the other lady.

"I'm Fiona Hart." She extended her hand.

"Pleased to meet you." He stole a quick look at the now empty porch stairs. "I gather those are the children's favorite cookies?"

"They are." The woman nodded. "Or at least they were when they stayed here last year. Lucy didn't mention it, but she made fresh sweet lemonade too. The children loved it during their last visit."

He nodded, not convinced Gavin was old enough to remember, but hopeful the flicker of light in Emily's eyes meant she did. "I know so little."

"The same can be said for parents of newborns. No one is handed a child with instructions. It will come together." Her hand landed on his forearm.

For the first time since that horrible phone call just over a week ago, Eric thought maybe she might be right. He looked to the back of the car and wondered if it would be all right to check in and take the luggage to their cabin or if he should wait to do that later and follow the children instead.

"They'll be fine with Lucy if you'd like to check in. My husband will come and get your bags."

Eric didn't mean to let his surprise show, but at the chuckle the lovely woman failed to suppress, he must have looked very surprised.

Not that he meant any offense, but the woman was most definitely old enough to be his… mother's older sister.

"Career military. The man could probably still march a fifty pound pack across Camp LeJeune in the dead of summer during a hunger strike."

"Make that one hundred pounds." Flanked by a dog at each side, a tall man with a full head of white hair and broad shoulders that shouted they'd done more than their share of work, appeared and shoved his hand at him. "General Hart."

Despite his current civilian status, Eric was overcome with the urge to salute.

"This is the young man using his sister's reservation," his wife said softly.

"Oh, yes." The man's booming voice lowered, the bright smile slipped. "Awfully sad business, all of that."

Awfully sad about covered it. As if confirming the consensus, one of the dogs stepped forward with one paw, stretched his neck and licked Eric's hand. He almost felt like smiling.

The General gave his dog a pat of approval and tipped his chin in his wife's direction. "You go with Fiona and she'll get you the keys."

"Under the circumstances, we thought it best to have you in a cabin closer to the main house. You'll still have the lovely view." Fiona waved him on. Eric hesitated, looking toward the back of the new SUV he'd bought. The General seemed to be hauling out the bags as if they were filled with feathers. By the time Eric turned back, Fiona was up the stairs and at the front door. He'd had to take the steps two at a time to catch up.

Inside, the main house was everything the exterior implied. Large dark wood pieces from centuries past took up space against light airy walls. Vases filled with fresh flowers shared space with bowls of fruits and colorful dishes of assorted candies.

Fiona made her way into the parlor, opened the drawer on a massive partners' desk and handed him a key. "Here you go."

"Don't I have to sign anything?"

"Why?" She smiled. "You're here, aren't you?"

"Well, uhm. Thank you." He supposed that was one way to look at it. He was indeed here and he had given his credit card number online. But for the first time since finding himself lost and confused, like Alice in Wonderland suddenly in a bizarre and unfamiliar world, he dared to hope this other worldly place might be his salvation.

CHAPTER TWO

"You've lost your mind!" wafted loudly from the kitchen. "I'm telling you," a pretty blonde with her hair twisted into a sloppy bun at the top of her head waved a finger at a shorter redheaded woman, "a dash of lemon is fantastic."

The petite redhead fisted her hands on her hips. "I am not, repeat not, putting lemon in my cannolis."

The firecracker blonde rolled her eyes. "You are so stubborn. Cannolis are Italian. I don't care what they taught you in that fancy French cooking school."

Eric was momentarily horrified at walking in on the argument. Not so much because he cared what the two were doing battle over, but because he had made such an effort to keep everything calm and peaceful for the children after their painfully stressful ordeal.

"Fine." The blonde whipped around. "Try and help." She waved her hands, palms up, at Lucy.

Leaning against the counters, popping what looked like donut holes into her mouth, a young woman in sweatpants and a baggy shirt with a whistle dangling from her neck pushed away from the cabinets and scissoring her arms like an umpire declaring the runner at home safe, looked from one woman to the other. "Not a problem. Do them both ways and I'll sacrifice myself for the taste testing."

The redhead sputtered and the blonde rolled her eyes.

"Okay. If not me, neutral territory." Whistle lady spun about and pointed at the two children seated at the end of the island watching the spat like spectators at a tennis match.

Eric had to do a double take. Chomping away at the pile of cookies in front of them, they were not horrified, upset, or complaining. They were riveted to the interaction. It was the most involved he'd seen them since they'd come through the double glass doors and into his life.

Yes, he decided. Time at Hart House was most definitely the

only smart decision he'd made so far.

• • • •

Iris loved her cousin Lily like a sister, but the girl was as protective of her recipes as a man was of his sports car. Heaven forbid anyone mess with either of their babies. Speaking of which. She turned her head to look at the two kids with enough cookies piled in front of them to feed an elementary school. What was the matter with parents today? Didn't they understand boundaries and limits were the foundation for responsible well balanced, and yes, happy children.

Scowling at her two cousins, Lily nudged the refrigerator door shut with her elbow, then turned to face the children. "Would you like to help choose the better cannoli?"

It took the little girl a moment to recognize Lily was talking to her. The child nodded quickly. Her little brother looked to his sister and did the same.

Iris had her doubts that either had any idea what a cannoli was. Reminding herself that it wasn't the children's fault their parents—with a little help from Lucy—didn't have a problem with putting their kids into a sugar coma, she sucked in a calming breath and did her best to plaster on a sincere smile for the children. After all, just because she'd spent the last few years dealing with spoiled rich kids didn't mean she had to take it out on these two. If anything, they looked a bit lost. "Have you ever had cannolis before?"

Clearly not sure of his answer, the younger sibling looked to his sister for guidance in responding. The young girl's mouth tightened and her brows dipped.

"Cannoli are an Italian pastry. Lily bakes a hard tubular shell then fills it with cream."

Immediately the little girl's face lit up, though the younger sibling still looked unsure.

"We need someone to tell us which recipe tastes better. Are you both up to the challenge?"

Like matching bookends, the two children nodded. Both had big button brown eyes and round faces with chubby cheeks. The little boy had curly golden locks, but the sister had chestnut, nearly pin straight shoulder length hair.

She knew of a few advertising companies that would kill for such an angelic looking pair of siblings.

"Very good, but if you're going to have extra dessert, then we won't want to spoil your dinner with all these cookies" She took hold of the plates, slowly easing them away, waiting for any signs of protest. When neither child reacted, she relaxed and quickly slid the dishes completely out of the way. "We'll have to get permission from your parents, but I'm sure if you eat all your supper they won't…"

At the sight of the young boy's lower lip trembling in unison with water pooling in the little girl's eyes, Iris's words faltered. She'd almost shoved the dish back in front of them, willing to offer them a dozen more cookies where those came from if they would only smile.

Lucy appeared instantly with a full pitcher of lemonade and forced cheer. Refilling the nearly empty glasses, she looked to Iris. "I made Emily and Gavin's favorite for tonight–spaghetti with meatballs. I'm sure if they eat all their dinner, their uncle won't mind a bit if they help you and Lily decide which recipe is the best."

Uncle? Feeling a chill, Iris noticed for the first time the tall brooding man in the doorway, staring daggers at her. The man pushed away from the wall and swaggered toward the island where both children had regained their composure and now stared almost curiously at the tall figure approaching them.

"I wonder if there's enough for me to offer an opinion. Born and raised in North Boston, you might say I know my cannoli." He smiled down at the children, but if Iris wasn't mistaken, the man looked more nervous than upset. Almost as if he expected to be told he wasn't welcome.

Waiting only a beat in silence, Lucy quickly answered, "The more the merrier."

"Are we expecting more guests?" Grams came into the room. Smiling brightly, she strolled around the island, placing a gentle hand on each child's shoulder. Instantly their stiff stance eased and though they didn't exactly smile, Iris could see they liked having Grams around. Smart kids. Everyone loved her. She might be a tad colorful and march to her own tune, but the woman had known how to show her grandchildren unconditional love.

"Nope." Lucy placed the pitcher on the counter. "Cannoli contest."

Grams raised one brow at Lucy and then shot her gaze over to Lily.

Shaking her head, Lily mumbled, "Don't ask."

Mr. Tall Dark and Brooding shifted his weight from one side to the other and Iris thought it seemed to take great effort for him to suck in a breath. "We should probably settle in before supper." He paused, his gaze lifting skyward a moment as though thinking through something important. "Wash up." He paused again. "Yes, wash up," he confirmed more to himself than anyone else.

"Good idea." Grams tapped the children lightly against the shoulder. "Iris, dear, why don't you show Mr. Johnson and the children to the Sycamore cabin?"

"Oh." Iris shot a quick glance from the two siblings to their uncle. She probably was the best qualified to deal with whatever family dynamic was underfoot. "Sure."

"I'm sure you're tired from your travels. Shall we set extra places for supper?" Grams asked.

Relief seemed to wash over the man's face, drawing some of the tension out of his shoulders. "Thank you. That would be very nice."

"Lovely." Grams leaned down and whispered to the children just loud enough for everyone to hear, but softly enough to feel like a secret. "This is my granddaughter, Iris. She's as nice as her name."

Both children scurried down from the benches. Emily glanced over her shoulder at Grams before taking hold of her brother's hand and slowly inching forward until the two stood in front of her. Iris had no idea what was going on. When she'd arrived late yesterday there had already been a crowd gathered playing cards. She'd stuck around long enough to be friendly, but not long enough to get an update on the current or expected guests.

"Nice to meet you. I'm Eric Johnson." Doing his best to sound relaxed and at ease, the stiffness in his stance and the shaky smile told Iris he was anything but. "Lead the way."

On the porch, Iris paused to point to the cabin only a stone's throw from the main house when she felt the tender warmth of a small hand bumping against hers. Pressed closely at her side, Emily kept her brother's hand tucked tightly in hers and easily slid her free hand into Iris's grasp.

Without hesitation, Iris folded her hand around the little girl's and only then did Emily look up, surprise shining in her eyes.

The same surprise was staring back at her in their uncle's huge whiskey brown eyes.

She'd have to teach him a thing or two about not reacting to the unexpected things kids did. Somewhere she was sure there was a secret childhood handbook that informed all children that surprise in an adult's face was a sign of weakness. The same handbook that told all toddlers to test a parent's worthiness by throwing a temper tantrum in the grocery store. Poor mom or dad who gave in had no idea that according to the secret handbook, they'd just lost the battle of wills for the remainder of their children's lives. "This cabin is one of the larger two bedrooms." She stepped off the porch. "There is a small kitchen with some basic supplies. You'll have to hit the One Stop if you plan to cook."

Another flash of surprise, teetering on panic, took over Eric's face. Whether it was at the need of buying groceries or the need to cook, or maybe just the idea of being alone with two children in a small cabin, she had no idea.

"This isn't the right house." The little girl frowned. "Ours had a blue door."

So they'd been here before. Since once again Iris had no idea what was going on, she didn't dare venture at offering a response. And frankly, these kids weren't in her charge. It wasn't her job to teach them to not be fussy about door colors. No matter how they looked at it, life would eventually be throwing them a lot bigger curves than red doors.

"Maybe it will be nice too," the uncle said.

The little girl couldn't be more than six but she had that who-are-you-kidding glare down pat. If her uncle didn't whither at the icy stare, maybe he was made of stronger stuff than Iris had given him credit for.

Using the key with the big red pom pom attached, he turned the lock and pushed the door open.

"I want my blue door." The young girl stopped in her tracks.

Weary brown eyes quickly scanned the contents of the small cabin, then bounced from Emily to Gavin, and finally to her. By the time their gazes met the man looked totally defeated.

Maybe these children weren't her responsibility, and maybe this man was clueless about how to handle children, but there was no point in letting him flounder in the wind at the children's expense. She took a step further into the room and pointed out the west window. "See that cabin across the garden?"

Slowly Emily followed the direction of the extended finger and nodded.

"That's where I'll be staying."

Emily cocked her head sideways and looked from Iris's parents' cabin back to the suitcases stacked by the door. For a few seconds, Iris thought for sure the little girl was going to insist once again on the blue door. Iris didn't even remember which cabin had a blue door.

"I like green." Emily took hold of her hand again. "Can we stay with you?"

CHAPTER THREE

Eric didn't know who was more surprised by Emily's request, him or Iris. For only a flash of a moment he spotted the startled look in the blonde's eyes before a curtain of indifference dropped, hiding whatever thoughts were going on in that pretty little head. And it was very pretty. Her grandmother had things half right. She might be nice but she was even more beautiful than her flower namesake.

"It's not nice to impose on people." The second the words had slipped from his lips he'd regretted them. Young eyes that had already been filled with sadness for so many days, now flared with pain. He might as well have told Emily he'd killed their puppy. Not that they had one. But the look stabbed his heart with the same precision as a surgeon's scalpel.

Nibbling on her lower lip, his niece backed away from him, angling herself behind a woman neither of them really knew. "I like green."

"Why don't we find a game for you and your brother to play while I take a minute to talk to your uncle?"

"We didn't bring anything to play with," Emily mumbled.

The censure in the eyes that flared in his direction almost caught him off guard. Iris couldn't be thinking anything worse than what he'd thought of himself a hundred times over since the lawyer's phone call. The bottom line was clear. Eric had no business raising children. No matter how much he wanted to do right by his sister, he knew more about raising tomatoes than he did about little boys and girls—and he knew pretty much squat about gardening.

"I packed your books," he said with more enthusiasm than the statement warranted. Especially since he was the only one excited about the books. As a child he'd loved the time spent on his parents' bed while his father read to him and Adele from his favorite books. By the time Eric was in elementary school he loved Louis L'Amour as much as his dad did. Neither Emily nor Gavin showed any interest in Eric's hardback editions, but that hadn't stopped him from taking the children to the last neighborhood bookstore in town to pick out a couple of age appropriate books.

"Books are good," Iris chimed in with an unexpected lilt of delight in her voice. "The American Girls were my favorite when I was your age. Nancy Drew too. What do you have?"

After only a moment of suspended silence, Eric crossed the room and quickly withdrew two large books from the overnight bag. "The woman at the store said these were some of her children's favorites."

Iris reached for the books, a sincere smile teasing at the corners of her mouth. "I loved the Berenstein Bears."

For the first time since he'd purchased the books, he saw a flicker of interest from his niece.

"Would you read it to us?" Emily asked.

Iris glanced up at him. If she was expecting him to give or deny permission, she'd be waiting a long time. He hadn't a clue what was or wasn't the right thing to do about any of this. As a matter of fact, Iris seemed to have a much better handle on the little ones than anyone he knew. Heaven knows from the way she'd glowered at him for not bringing games it was rather obvious that she didn't agree with the psychologist's advice not to overwhelm them with toys as substitutes for their loss. The stern older man had made such a strong argument against toys that Eric had felt miserably guilty buying the books, but he simply didn't know what else to do. Except coming here. He shrugged at the woman who had bonded with the children with few words in only a few minutes.

"Let's do this." Iris hunched down to be even with the children.

Had Eric seen anyone else do that? His mind wandered to how would he feel if he were scared, alone, and forced to talk to a man towering at least four feet above him. He really was an idiot.

"Let's get your bags, take them to your room, and put the clothes away. Then we'll go back to the big house, and after supper we'll read both the books." Iris glanced from one child to the other, waiting for a response. "The cabin should have some games and puzzles here for later, but if you'd like, we might hunt around at my grandmother's to see if she still has any of the books from when I was a child."

Emily didn't take long to consider her words. Letting go of her brother's hand, she nodded at Iris and then walked to the small bag that held her and Gavin's clothes.

Studying the small suitcase a moment, Iris looked at the slightly larger bag beside it and then turned to face him. "Is this all their things?"

He nodded. What more could he do? He'd been rather surprised with the small amount of belongings that had—or hadn't—come with the children. According to the solicitor someone on the continent would be shipping more of their belongings. He simply didn't know what or when.

"Very well, we have a job to do." Iris clapped her hands together and smiled down at the two little people. "Let's get cracking."

Without hesitation the two kids moved toward their room.

A step behind his niece and nephew, Eric couldn't help but follow along. Somehow she'd turned unpacking a bag into a game and within minutes all their clothes were neatly folded in drawers or hung in the closet. She'd made it look so very easy. He'd give anything to understand how she'd done that. Anything.

● ● ● ●

There were several things Iris was sure of. First, Uncle Eric didn't have a clue about the children. Jumping to the second conclusion, that surely he hadn't been caring for these kids very long, came easily. The next obvious thing was that these two little ones were as outside of their comfort zone as their uncle. And since invitations for guests to join the family for dinner in the main dining room were few and far between, it was clear that Iris's grandmother and Lucy knew more than she did about these people. All she needed was to call on a bit of patience and a few minutes alone with them to get caught up to speed. Even though she'd taken her grandfather's advice to heart and now had all the time in the world, well, at least until her savings ran out, as far as gathering the inside scoop on Uncle Eric and his charges was concerned, sooner would be preferable to later.

Hair clipped in a loose ponytail, Iris's cousin Callie set a massive salad bowl on the table while chatting away with her sister Poppy.

Lily was still slaving away in the kitchen and neither Cindy nor Lily's fiancé were going to make it tonight. Still, Iris was pleased to spend time with any of her cousins. Ever since informing Mrs. Belton that it was time she raised her own children, Iris had been savoring the idea of some much needed one on one time with her cousins in the peaceful and child free zone of Hart Land.

Tonight, the only item on her agenda was catching up on all the happenings on the lake. For years she could spend months without coming by to visit and all of a sudden, every time she turned around another of her cousins had fallen in love and turned the family dynamics on its ear. She wouldn't be at all surprised if pretty soon there was a whole slew of next generation Harts to be corralled.

Grams strolled into the room, set a gravy boat down, then a dish of meatballs, and took her seat at the opposite end of the table from where the General always sat. "Everything all right, dear?"

"Oh, yes. Of course." Reaching for the back of her chair, the warm strength of Eric's hand brushed against hers. Both had gone to pull her seat out at the same time. The small static shock that sparked at the momentary connection had her drawing back.

Nonplussed by the contact, Eric continued to retract her seat for her, then when she remained rooted in place, waved her into the chair.

"Thank you." It had been a while since the simple courtesy her grandfather and father had always shown the women in their lives had been bestowed on her.

With a quick smile and nod, Eric turned to peruse the remaining seats. Sarge, one of the retrievers, sauntered away from the General and nudged him until he almost fell into the seat beside Iris.

"I was just about to suggest you sit beside my granddaughter." Her grandmother waved in his direction. "Gavin can sit beside you and Emily beside Iris."

"Oh." Iris popped up from her seat. "I can move down one."

"Nonsense." Her grandmother gestured for her to sit again. "Eric has had a long drive today. This way Emily is between you and me, and Poppy can get to know Gavin."

Bless her cousin Poppy, she smiled at both kids and immediately tapped the seat beside her. "I love a chance to sit next to a handsome young man."

Gavin blinked, studied her for a moment and then must have decided being called a handsome young man wasn't too bad a thing as he crawled up into his seat and let Poppy splay the napkin across his lap.

On the other hand, Emily seemed to think twice between sitting in the seat her uncle had pulled out for her and staying close to her little brother. Slowly lowering herself into the chair, she kept her gaze fixed on Gavin.

"Here we are!" Lucy carried a large bowl of spaghetti in each hand, setting one down at either end of the table.

On her heels, Aunt Virginia followed with a massive salad bowl and a bright smile. The woman had worked long and hard hours at the funeral parlor ever since inheriting it from her husband and yet, she always had a smile. "I hope everyone is hungry. As usual, there's enough food to feed an army."

Lucy spun around. "Bread coming right up. Lily baked it."

Eric sniffed the air like a thoroughbred pup, not sure when the woman had time to bake cannolis and bread. "My sainted grandmother couldn't compete with this."

Smothering a smile, Grams shook her head at him. "A touch of the blarney?"

"Nope. One hundred percent Italian. Mom's side from Milan and Dad's from a small town near Lake Como. Two families within spitting distance and they had to meet in Boston."

"Isn't that always the case," the General chimed in.

"Certainly was for Keith and me." Aunt Virginia reached for the butter, her gaze softening at the mention of her husband's name. "Growing up in a small town like Lawford and we had to go all the way to Fordham University to fall in love with each other. All because of the most boring statistics class."

"I suppose it's a good thing it wasn't an interesting class or you might have paid attention to the teacher instead of each other," Grams teased, and Aunt Virginia swallowed a knowing smile.

"Sorry, lost track of time." Lily rushed into the room with another platter of small rolls.

"Are we still going to taste the desserts?" Emily asked.

"Yes, ma'am." Lily smiled at her then shifted her gaze to her cousin. "And I know which one you're going to pick too."

Iris harrumphed, then smothered a chuckle. There was more than one way to get Lily to double bake dessert.

"How long will you be staying with us, Mr. Johnson?" Grams asked.

"Eric, please." His gaze shifted to his niece and nephew. "I'm not sure yet."

The General glanced up at him. "You don't need to return to work any time soon?"

"No sir." Eric may have responded to her grandfather's question, but his eyes tracked the bowl of pasta passed around on his end of the table, occasionally diverting to his niece's plate and back.

The poor man was more than out of his element. If she was reading him correctly, he was debating what to do with the bowl when it finally came his way. The man was in serious need of a crash course in parenting. What the heck was their story?

She might as well lead the way here too. "Gavin, do you want to serve yourself or shall I?"

The plate dangled from Iris's hand and Gavin studied it a long moment and then sputtered, "You."

From the seat beside her she could feel Eric exhale with relief.

"You must have a nice boss to give you plenty of time to… adjust." Grams barely glanced up from twirling pasta onto her fork.

Eric nodded. "I'm actually an independent contractor. I can take or turn down any offers of work I get. This seems a good time to lay low."

"Yes. I can see why." Grams nodded. "Exactly what do you do?"

"I work in the oil and gas industry."

"Oh." Grams' brow furrowed in thought. "Is there much work for you around here?"

"Not exactly. I usually work on oil rigs."

Iris watched the children. Neither seemed particularly interested in their uncle's job description. The way they attacked their dinner, anyone would think they hadn't eaten in years.

"Must be exciting work?" the General asked, a twinkle in his eyes.

"Certainly never boring." Eric measured his niece's progress on her meal. "I could be working one week in the North Sea and the next in the Gulf of Mexico."

Grams frowned. "That doesn't sound very practical for a family man."

The color drained from Eric's face and his gaze dragged from one child to the other. "No, ma'am. Not very."

Not very. Iris followed his gaze and could almost feel the depth of pain in his eyes. What the heck was the whole story?

CHAPTER FOUR

T he last thing Eric wanted at this moment was to leave what had become the safety of Hart House. Dinner had gone off without a hitch. By the grace of God, it turned out the kids' favorite meal was on his short list of foods he could actually prepare. Especially if the recipe involved opening a can and heating its contents. He'd mastered grilled cheese sandwiches and canned tomato soup in college and tweaked it to perfection through the years by substituting brie or gruyere, depending on the contents of his fridge.

He'd tried coaxing Emily and Eric with pizza, hamburgers, and in desperation, his favorite boxed mac and cheese. None had worked; they'd barely picked at their meals, until tonight. Perhaps it hadn't been the food but the person preparing it. Or the place. Or maybe the beautiful woman sitting beside them as they ate. Had Iris served him fried bugs in prune juice, he would have most likely cleaned his plate for one of her approving smiles. She'd yet to bestow one on him, and much to his surprise, he found himself very much wanting one. Beautiful women were not an anomaly for him. Since high school, he'd mastered the art of making a woman happy. No matter the age, remember the small stuff, ask them to dance, and it never hurts to bring flowers. Still, not since his first crush in junior high had he felt so out of his league. Then again, right now everything in his life from the children, to Iris, to getting up in the morning to face another day seemed out of his league. *Oh, Adele.*

After tonight, another thing he suspected was that cannoli would be the kids' favorite dessert, and thank heaven available in great abundance at just about any bakery within spitting distance of his place. Standing at either side of the children, Iris and Lily waited patiently as the entire table watched the two children devouring the first then second pastry.

How they'd had room for not one but two cannoli baffled Eric.

"Well?" Lily asked.

As usual, Gavin looked to his sister to take the lead. Emily, on the other hand, had looked thoughtfully skyward, pursing and smacking her lips, dragging the moment on.

For a few brief moments he'd understood what it felt like to be able to cut the tension in the room with a knife.

"I think," Emily smiled, "I like them both. Maybe we could do this again tomorrow to decide?"

"Ha." The General let out a loud burst of laughter. "Diplomat in the making. And a smart one at that."

"Agreed." Iris smiled at the little girl and dug into her own dessert.

Eric had to admit he could barely taste the difference. He wasn't sure he could have picked a winner either.

"I think you've been playing longer than you let on." The older man named Ralph, who if Eric had his introductions straight, was a neighbor, teasingly chided Gavin for jumping his men with double kings.

The two had been playing checkers while some locals and the General played a card game of Whist, and Mrs. Hart and Emily tinkered with paints on a canvas. He definitely did not want to leave the family porch and brave the night alone with the kids in the cabin.

"Found them." Iris pulled the screen door open and let it slam shut behind her. "I knew there was no way Mom would throw out the classics."

"Classics?" Eric asked.

"First chapter books. My sister and I would read these for hours. At least until I discovered Nancy Drew." Iris let the pile land with a thud on an empty square table.

"Those are in the new library nook on the second floor." Without looking up, Fiona Hart tipped her head toward the inside of the house. When no one responded, still focusing on the painting in front of her, the woman continued, "The Nancy Drew, dear."

"Right." Iris nodded then looked at her watch and turned to Eric, but said nothing.

He'd have to be an idiot not to realize what she wasn't saying. He'd noticed over half an hour ago that he should be putting the kids to bed, but with Iris having wandered off and the children looking the most entertained and, well, normal that he'd seen them since picking them up at the airport, he didn't have the heart to call an end to the day. Until now. "It's getting late. We should hit the road."

Two heads spun in his direction before sharp gazes turned downcast. Without protest, both children stood and walked in his direction. He'd have preferred argumentative attitudes to such downtrodden expressions.

When Gavin reached where Iris stood, he paused and looked up. "Are you still going to read to us?"

Iris reached out and tousled the boy's curly hair. "You bet. One Berenstein Bears and then one of my favorites. Huckleberry Finn."

He wouldn't say that happiness overtook either of the children, but thanks to Iris they were making greater strides in hours than they had in days.

Hugging a pile of books to her chest, Iris led the way to the cabin with the red door. This time there were no complaints about door colors or cabins. Once inside, Emily hurried down the short hall.

"Go on," Iris encouraged Gavin. "Follow your sister. Brush your teeth, then put on the pajamas we laid out for tonight."

Gavin nodded and trotted off after Emily.

"How many children do you have?" Eric asked.

Shaking her head, Iris turned around to face him. "None. Pretty much anyone who has ever babysat would know how to put kids to bed, but as it so happens, I'm a nanny."

At least he didn't feel so stupid knowing less about childrearing than a professional childcare person. Though she was right. Most teenagers would probably be better with the children than he was, but it wasn't his fault that parents frowned upon asking teenage boys to be in charge of keeping their children out of trouble. Though now that he thought about it, asking an adult bachelor wasn't a much safer bet.

"All clean." Emily came racing in front of Iris and flashed a large toothy grin.

So that was how it worked? Obviously Emily was already familiar with the routine but had failed to fill him in on it.

"Looks good." Iris flashed that smile he was learning to like. A lot. "Get into your PJs and I'll introduce you to Tom Sawyer and Huck Finn."

Emily eagerly led the way, her brother only a step behind her, and Eric fell into step behind Iris. In no time she had both children snuggled under the covers and waved Eric in for a short bedtime prayer, a kiss on the cheek, and a wish that Adele were here instead of him

Seated in the rocker tucked into a corner of the room, Iris began reading from the hardcover classic while Eric watched, perched against the doorway. In no time, both little ones lost the battle with the weight of their eyelids.

Slipping a postcard into the pages to mark her place, Iris closed the tome and set it down on the side table. "Do they sleep through the night?"

"For the most part."

"Good." Iris brushed a lock of hair away from Gavin's face and sucking in a deep breath, left the room. Waiting for the click of the door latching shut behind them, she folded her arms across her chest. "One question?"

Eric nodded.

"Are their parents coming home?"

He shook his head and she blew out a heavy sigh.

"I was afraid of that." She pinched the bridge of her nose and seemed to be contemplating the next step in gaining world peace. Or how to turn a dunce like him into a competent parent.

Personally, he'd have gone with solving world peace as the easier problem.

"Do you cook?"

"Some."

Another sigh escaped. "Cold cereal doesn't count."

"In that case, not so much. But I can make spaghetti."

She bobbed her head. "Okay. I'll tell Lucy that you'll be joining us for breakfast tomorrow—"

"The website—"

"I know, but the cottages don't include dinner either. She'll be happy to feed the children. Lucy lives for the chance to fatten people up. I swear, she had more to do with Lily's fabulous desserts than the school in Paris. Anyhow, after breakfast you should hit the One Stop. Pick up some staples. If you'd like I can give you a few fool-proof recipes for the kitchen challenged that will keep your niece and nephew from starving."

He nodded again. "That would be nice. Thank you. I mean, I'm sure I could find some recipes on the internet but this would be better." Besides, the kids already felt comfortable with her. And so did he. "Will you give me a list for the store?"

She looked from him to the closed bedroom door and back. "I'll do you one better. After breakfast, while Lucy is putting the kids into another sugar coma, and Grams cons Emily into helping her sort paints or something, you and I will hit the store."

"Thank you." Based on the last few hours—days, actually—he had a feeling he would be saying that a lot. If he thought Hart House could be the answer he'd been looking for, the General's granddaughter could be his salvation.

• • • •

Funny, as much as Iris had rushed to escape the trappings of caring for someone else's children, and as reluctant as she might have been to get involved with another pair of siblings, now standing outside the not-blue-door cabin, she was finding it hard to walk away. With every step, even knowing the children were soundly asleep, she couldn't shake the need to turn back and stand over them. Like a newborn parent, she felt compelled to make sure they were still breathing. She didn't have a clue what the story was behind this odd new family— and she was quite sure it was very new—but the depth of sadness in those two precious faces nearly broke her heart.

"How did it go?" Pad and pencil in hand, Grams lifted her gaze to Iris.

The screen door slammed shut behind her and it took a few deep breaths of her Grams lilac lotion to soothe her soul and find the words. "They're asleep."

Ralph the neighbor, who was as much a part of this family since his retirement as any blood relative, played a card and picked up the trick. "Nasty shame that whole business."

"Poor little ones," Louise Franklin, the town crier, muttered softly, shaking her head. "You hear about this sort of thing all the time, but it really hits home when you see the loved ones left behind."

Iris sank into the rocker beside her grandmother. "What exactly happened?"

"Skiing accident. In Chamonix." The General shuffled the deck.

"France?" Iris asked

Her grandfather nodded. "I seem to remember his family owned a home there."

"Yet they vacationed here before?" Iris knew that from her conversation with Emily, but most of the families she'd known who could afford both the time and money to ski in the French Alps, never mind own a home there, were not the sort to vacation at a family establishment on Lawford Mountain.

"Oh, yes." Grams laid her sketchpad down and reached for a piece of Lily's Mandel bread to dip in the hot chocolate beside her. "The children's mother, Adele, was a lovely lady. She so loved coming back to nature. By the time they'd left, her husband had even come around to enjoying the simpler side of life."

"Makes no sense to me why anybody would want to go all the way across the ocean to ski when we have perfectly good mountains right here." Ralph sorted his cards.

Louise rolled her eyes. "I love this mountain just as much is you do, but who wouldn't want to go to France?"

"Me, for one." Ralph closed his cards. "I bid two."

"I bid three, and you are not normal." Louise looked more closely at her cards, shaking her head, then glanced back up. "So, is this nice young man related to the mother or the father?"

Grams blew on the chocolate liquid in her cup. "Eric is Adele's brother."

So the poor man had inherited two kids he clearly didn't know what to do with and lost his sister at the same time. "He doesn't seem very comfortable with the children."

"Few bachelors are." Grams dipped the cookie in her cup again.

"That's true," Iris nodded reluctantly, "but I would expect an uncle to be a bit more familiar with the children."

Grams gently nibbled on the last bite of the cookie and shrugged. Her grandmother was the embodiment of the old adage if you can't say something nice don't say anything at all. Although usually she always found something nice to say. The woman's silence served to show that Iris wasn't the only one who thought the man had a surprisingly distant relationship with the two children he was now responsible for. From what she could see, they all might as well have been strangers.

"I think his efforts are admirable," Ralph added. "It's not easy taking on parenting when there are two parents, never mind a bachelor whose job keeps him out on oil rigs."

Iris supposed that would explain why he wasn't close to his sister's children. Working on an oil rig in the ocean would make Sunday night dinners a challenge. "Are there any more siblings?"

"I don't know," Grams answered at the same time the General said, "No," then looked up from his game to see Grams and Iris looking at him. "I forget who mentioned it but there are no other siblings. After all, if there were I don't suppose that poor man would be trying to take on an instant family without more help."

And the man was definitely going to need help and if the last few hours was any indication, for the sake of the children, she had a pretty good idea who that help was going to be.

"I'm heading home. Have to be at the bakery bright and early." Lily came through the doorway, her face lighting up at mention of her new business. "I made an extra batch of double butter croissants for breakfast tomorrow and some blueberry scones. Lucy reminded me that Emily enjoyed my scones last year."

For the family, one of the perks of Lily being engaged to a fireman was his long shifts. So far she spent almost as much time baking at Hart House as she did in her own bakery. Snatching a cookie from the plate between her and her grandmother, Iris pushed to her feet. "I'll walk down hill with you." She should try and get a decent night's sleep. Tomorrow had every sign of becoming a very long day.

CHAPTER FIVE

In the short time Eric had been with the children, morning rituals had been a chore at best. Neither child seemed in any hurry to eat, dress, or talk to him. This morning had been a bit of an eye opener on the possibilities for normal. He'd woken up bright and early expecting to either find them still asleep or in their pajamas, huddled quietly. Instead he was greeted by the sight of each child on the sofa, fully dressed, perusing the pages of a book.

Not for the first time, he wasn't quite sure what to make of it, other than whatever he done before, he hadn't done it right. "Is anyone besides me hungry?"

Both children looked up. First Emily nodded, and then, sure of his sister's response, clutching his cheetah to his side, so did Gavin. For just a beat, he waited for the customary "I want to go home" comment. By the time both children were standing at the front door holding hands, he realized something important had shifted.

"Mrs. Hart was telling me last night that Lucy is one of the best cooks in the county. Breakfast should be a real treat." He wasn't quite sure what to say to the kids; he was never sure what to say to the children. Heck, half the time he wasn't sure what to say to adults. Small talk was not his gift. Especially when whomever he was talking to didn't talk back. Right about now he'd settle for a nod of acknowledgment.

"Oh, there you are!" Lucy came hurrying through the front door to greet them on the porch. "I knew you were early risers. I just set breakfast out. I made my special French toast casserole and I even have a surprise for you."

Emily's eyes widened and for just a second the corners of her mouth twitched, almost breaking into a smile. "Chocolate chip pancakes?"

"You are a smart girl. I can't fool you."

This time, a hint of a smile graced Emily's lips. He should have known to try pancakes. As a kid he had loved when his mom made cookie-cutter pancakes. His reward for not fussing when she ran a lot of errands would be to stop and go through the extra-large cookie-cutter section and pick out a new shape for his pancakes. Sometimes for a cookie. He'd forgotten about that until now. The memory was almost enough to make him smile.

Lucy rubbed her hands together and gestured for the children to follow her.

Inside, the General sat at one end of the table, a dog on either side of him, and Mrs. Hart at the opposite end. He had hoped to find Iris there as well. In only a few hours he'd grown to appreciate her innate ability to recognize what the kids needed, and steer them in the right direction. Then again, he was a fast learner. Taking in the buffet set up on the side board, he walked with the children to the opposite side of the room and picking up a plate, looked to Emily. "Do you want to serve yourself or would you like me to help you?"

Emily slowly perused everything on the buffet. From left to right, her gaze lingered on the chocolate chip pancakes. He should have known. His mom had nothing on Lucy. Stars, gingerbread men, or was that a snowman?

Didn't matter, Emily reached for the plate and held it in front of the pancakes. "I'll have three, please."

He didn't understand why, but it pleased him enormously that she let him help. Not that he hadn't tried since the day he picked her up at the airport, but somehow, this felt different.

"I see we're already indulging." Iris came walking into the room, a bright smile on her face. She paused at her grandmother, leaned in to kiss her on the cheek before joining them at the buffet. "I slept like the proverbial log. How about you guys? Did you have a good night sleep?"

Emily nodded first, then Gavin followed his sister's lead.

"Good morning, Lady." Iris scratched the scruff of the golden retriever's neck.

So intent on serving Emily what she wanted quickly so he could take care of his nephew, Eric hadn't noticed when the two dogs had come to sit at the children's side, never mind recognize which dog was which. "How can you tell them apart?"

Iris stepped around Gavin to scratch the other dog a moment with one hand, and ran her fingers gently across the back of the little boy's curls. "I'd like to say there's a big secret to it, but Sarge has a small diamond patch of white on his chest and Lady is all blonde."

The one with the diamond patch, Sarge, sat staring at Gavin, a rough looking tennis ball between his paws. Still holding cheetah with one hand securely on his lap, when Gavin leaned over to pick the ball up, the General cleared his throat. "He's always looking for someone to play fetch, but not in the house. You can take that outside and play with him later."

Gavin nodded and flashed the pup an apologetic glance before digging back into his food with his free hand.

"Heaven help me, the coffee pot broke down at the house." Poppy hurried into the room, bypassing her grandparents, then doubling back, quickly kissed each on the cheek before practically diving for the coffee in the corner. "We have an early elders meeting at church. They want the entire staff there and even earlier than usual."

The General shook his head. "Good thing you never joined the Corps."

Swallowing a long gulp of the hot brew, Poppy smiled over her shoulder at the older man. "No argument from me there, sir. I love you, but early to bed early to rise is one gene I did not inherit." Topping off the cup, she put a croissant on a plate and hurried to take a seat across the table.

As much as he enjoyed pancakes, the smell of freshly cooked bacon, and what he presumed must have been Lucy's French toast casserole, had him loading his plate, leaving no room for childhood memories of cookie cutter pancakes. Ready to sit, somehow the dogs had done it again. Sarge banked left and steered Gavin toward the General, and Lady moved Emily towards Mrs. Hart, leaving him and Iris in between his niece and nephew once again.

"Do you have any plans for today?" Mrs. Hart asked.

"As a matter of fact," Eric unfolded his napkin on his lap, "I need to hit the grocery store."

Iris took a seat beside him. "I thought I'd run him over to the One Stop for a few things. Perhaps the children could stay here with you?"

"Of course, we don't want to impose," Eric said hurriedly. Everyone had been so nice to him so far, he didn't want to wear out his welcome before his day really started.

"Nonsense. We don't get many chances to spend time with children. I have just the new project for us." Mrs. Hart dabbed the corners of her mouth with a napkin and turned to face Emily. "Do you like to paint?"

Emily bobbed her head enthusiastically. "Yes. My teacher, Mrs. Henry, says I'm very good. Mama always puts my pictures on the refrigerator."

Any joy the project held slipped at the reminder of the loss of her mother. She tipped her chin up and blinked back watery eyes. The brave front reminded him so much of Adele. Not so much the adult who had adapted so well to her husband's lifestyle, but the little girl who'd insisted she could play ball with her big brother, or refused to wear a dress if her big brother didn't have to, or who graduated top of her class in mechanical engineering, beating out her big brother.

Those are the moments that hit Eric the hardest. But of all the things he'd lost through the years, the right to grieve for his sister had to take a backseat to her children. He owed Adele that much. No matter what, these children and their broken hearts would have to come first.

• • • •

There were a great many things that Iris loved about the lake. The One Stop and Katie O'Leary had been two of them since she was old enough to remember the delightful redhead and her lovely Irish lilt. For a lot of years, Iris thought the woman was an angel. Sometimes she still did.

"Top of the morning to you." Katie popped up from behind the counter, smiling at Iris as though she'd come in carrying the Holy Grail.

"And the rest of the day to you!" Of all the exotic places Iris had travelled with the families she worked for, she had yet to set foot on the Emerald Isle. Visiting Ireland was on the top of her bucket list.

Maybe now that she had some free time on her hands she could go. Of course, logic said what she really needed now was a new job.

"And who do we have here?" Wiping her hands on the side of her jeans, Katie came out of the aisle and smiled up at Eric.

"Eric Johnson." He extended his hand. "A guest at Hart House."

"Ah." Katie cast a brief glance in Iris's direction. "Hart House seems to be doubly blessed with handsome guests lately. You wouldn't be married now, would you?"

Eric chuckled softly and flashed a smile at Katie that almost made Iris's knees buckle. "No, ma'am. A bachelor through and through."

And just like that, he must have remembered he might still be a bachelor, but one with major responsibilities. As quickly as the smile took over his face, it fell away, replaced by the sad reality of recent events.

"Well. What can I do for you two?"

Eric looked around the small neighborhood store.

A wide array of dry and fresh goods mixed with tackle and bait, and of course, boating supplies, made perfect sense for a store on the lake with a long wooden dock. In the summer there was nothing unusual about driving up to the dock in a boat, running in for whatever a person needed and heading back out to open water. For her, that would have been candy and chocolates as a kid and later when she was more grown up, beer or wine. His gaze seemed to land on the fishing gear.

"Do you fish, Eric?" Katie asked.

"Not since I was a kid." He ran his hand up one fishing rod in particular. "My dad had a rod that looked a lot like this one."

"Popular color. Good sturdy pole. With all the fresh water creeks around here, we sell quite a lot of that one."

Eric nodded and turned to the canned goods section. "What I really need is some staples to cook decent meals for our stay here."

"And how long will that be?"

The question gave him pause. Though they hadn't discussed it yet, Iris had the feeling this man was running on a wing and a prayer because beyond any doubt, he did not have a plan. "Our reservation is for one week."

Katie gave a quick dip of her chin, but said nothing more.

Referencing the recipes Iris had printed out for him, he walked about gathering the items on the list. Iris started out at his side, but quickly realized the man might not have been a gourmet chef but he at least knew his way around a grocery list.

"There's a sadness in those eyes," Katie said softly, wrapping up some soda bread. "Lucy asked for some extra loaves."

"Sounds like we're having corned beef and cabbage for dinner."

"That it does." Katie placed the bread in a bag and glanced up at the man carefully reading his list. "If any place—or any one—can bring some sunshine back into those eyes it would be you folks at Hart House."

While Iris appreciated Katie's confidence in her family, she was pretty sure that it would take a lot more than Lily's baking or Gram's smile to make what was wrong with that new family right again.

"You know," she sidled up closer to Iris, "a good woman can do miracles for a troubled man."

"That may be true, but it sounds like you've been spending too much time with Lucy and her matchmaking notions."

"I'm just saying the right woman can do wonders for a broken heart."

"It's not what you're thinking. This situation is going to need more than a good woman."

Katie shrugged, smiled, and handed Iris the bag. "Never underestimate the power of a good woman."

CHAPTER SIX

"Got it, Grams. Thanks." Iris slipped her phone into her pocket. "Everything is going well at the house. Grams suggested we take a quick detour through town, stop at Lily's bakery and pick up something special for dessert at lunchtime."

A big part of Eric wanted to head back to check on the kids, but another part of him liked the idea of a little more time where he didn't have to question his every thought and action. "Lead the way."

In the General's Jeep, Iris turned onto the main road. Lawford wasn't a very large place, he'd known that from his quick Internet map search. In only a few minutes the town's short Main Street came into view.

"We can do a quick drive to the end and back, or if you're up to it, we can park here and walk it."

"Walking would be good. I've neglected my regular workout routine ever since I found out about Adele. I'm going to have to figure out how to fit that back into my routine sooner than later. And eventually, if I want to pay the bills, I'm going to have to return to work."

Iris swung into the nearest parking spot in front of the Pastry Stop and hopped out of the car. "You mentioned you worked on oil rigs."

"Pretty much." He slammed his door shut. "I work on any ocean-based machinery. There are only a few of us—"

"Iris! What a pleasant surprise!" A slender brunette wearing some kind of frock stuttered to a halt in front of his tour guide. "I thought you were in Thailand. Oh no, wait, India. Riding elephants. It sounds so exciting! I'm green with envy."

A plastic smile slid across Iris's face, quickly erasing the momentary grimace. "Yes, India. And where are you rushing off to?"

A genuine smile took over the brunette's face. "The bakery, of course. Business has just been booming at the Cut 'N Curl ever since I started serving Lily's croissants and mandels in the morning and her brownies and cookies in the afternoon. It's only 10:30 and I'm already out of everything."

"I am so glad to hear that." This time Iris's face lit up with a genuine smile.

The bubbly woman looked down at her watch. "I hate to run but Mrs. Norton's perm is going to time out in fifteen minutes so I have to hurry."

Iris waved as the woman rushed passed them into the pastry shop, and pivoted around to walk up the street.

"Cut and curl? Salon?" he asked.

"Yep. Betty bought the place a few years ago." Iris waved an arm to the right as they approached a blinking pink neon sign. "This is Mabel's Diner. Best home-cooked food after Lucy's."

"I'll remember that. I don't suppose they deliver?"

Iris chuckled. "You're going to have to go back to Boston for that."

He nodded, taking in the small shops, slowing down as they reached the spinning barber pole. Inside he recognized the General playing checkers with Ralph. Glancing upward, he bit back a laugh at the storefront name. "Floyd's?"

"That's right." She grinned up at the sign and tossed him an I-dare-you-to-say-something-about-it stare.

He'd learned a lot about women and communicating with just a look. Not willing to take the silent challenge, he opted for a simple and hopefully safe question. "And what's the barber's name?"

"That would be Floyd." Her shoulders relaxed and she waved at the men inside and turned away to continue walking. "Sort of."

"Sort of?" He quickened his gate to catch up to her.

"Basically, he bought the barber shop from Floyd. There was so much nostalgia attached to this place having the same name as the popular 60's TV show with Andy Griffith, that not only did the shop keep the name, but so did the barber."

In an odd way that sort of made sense. Singers and actors took on stage names all the time. "So what's his real name?"

Iris waved her arms open. "Haven't a clue. I'm not sure anybody does."

"Really." He smiled at the man's efforts. "I suppose he won't be the first or the last person to succeed on the heels of a great marketing ploy." They reached the end of the shops and he slowed his pace at the sound of children in the nearby playground. The old-fashioned park with a carousel and tall metal slide took him back to years ago when he and his sister lived for an afternoon in the park.

"I've always loved the sound of children's laughter." Iris paused beside him. "I can't imagine what it must be like to lose a sister."

"In some ways I lost her a long time ago. We're only two years apart. As kids we were inseparable. Once school started we fell into the typical big brother little sister roles, but stayed close nonetheless. Once we hit college, life seemed to get between us." Or at least Richard had. "She met her husband my last year at school. She was a sophomore. Richard had a charming British accent and proceeded to sweep her off her feet. It didn't hurt that he had the money to go with the accent. She was invited to summer with his family."

"Which meant she didn't spend her summers with your family." Iris sat at a picnic table and patted the bench beside her for him to do the same.

Straddling the bench, he kept his eyes on a pair of siblings running back and forth. "Mom had passed away from cancer Adele's senior year of high school. Dad couldn't take being in the house alone, so he sold it and moved to Florida near my mom's dad. The two had always gotten along well and shared a love for Mom and her memory. My work as soon as I graduated college took me everywhere. No time to sulk over the memories in the house. I suppose traveling with Richard made it easier for her as well. Neither of us had to go home and face Mom not being there."

"I'm sorry for your loss."

He bobbed his head. Whether she meant Adele or his mother he wasn't quite sure. "By the time they decided to get married, I don't think I liked Richard any more than Richard liked us. Deep inside I always thought he looked down on our blue-collar family. Dad was an electrician. We had a comfortable middle-class life. But it didn't compare with his family. I always expected to see his eyes cross looking down his nose at us."

Iris didn't say anything, she just listened. He didn't realize until now how badly he needed to have somebody just listen.

"If we saw each other ten times over the last ten years that was a lot." And just as much his fault as his sister's. He certainly couldn't blame Richard for that. "I guess it never occurred to me that she wouldn't always be there. That we wouldn't have another day, another year, another time to make things right."

"You wouldn't be unique in that. Most of us expect to have a tomorrow."

He tore his gaze away from the children he'd been watching, and looked at her. "I don't want to screw this up."

She seemed to be considering his words. Possibly looking for an easy way to let him know he already had, or maybe searching for words of encouragement, or perhaps wondering the same thing he was…why in heaven's name had his sister left a bachelor like him with her two children. "I wish I had some easy answers for you. All you can do is your best. Follow a few basic rules."

"Like?"

"At this age, routine is important. Standard bedtime. Not too much sugar. Creative activities. Limited screen time."

"Screen time? They're little."

"Exactly." She nodded. "And maybe you have better instincts than most parents nowadays who hand their toddlers a tablet and let the screen entertain them. You knew to buy them books instead."

He held back a scoff; he hadn't known a blasted thing, but he had to try something. "My sister's attorney had strict instructions. Starting with if anything happened to Adele and Richard the kids were to be packed up and shipped off before his parents got wind of what had happened. Another thing was for us to have counseling. I suppose she knew how hard this would be for everyone. I'd barely picked the children up from the airport when I was given the name of a psychologist and an appointment time for the next morning. You have no idea how hard it was for me to ignore his advice and buy the children a few books."

"First, he was clearly an idiot." She offered a reassuring smile. "And defying him shows you have good instincts."

A woman pushing an infant in a stroller called to the two children he'd kept an eye on as they circled around after each other, giggling and laughing. A moment later "time to go" crossed the mother's lips and the duo hurried to her side. The pair looked to be a little younger than Emily and Gavin.

So many thoughts and fears swirled around in his head. He couldn't help but wonder would he ever see his niece and nephew laughing and playing as carefree as the children now chatting away at their mother's side?

• • • •

"The day seems to have flown by." Lucy wiped a pot dry and set it aside. "I think the children really enjoyed themselves."

Fiona Hart nodded. "Emily did well with the paints. Gavin is still hesitant."

"At least they seem to have a good appetite." Iris handed Lucy another pan from dinner.

"How did the visit into town go?" Grams placed one of the dry pots into the cupboard. "I'm concerned for Eric too."

"Yes," Iris nodded at her grandmother, "you can see how hard all of this is for him. I think you may be right. He's ignoring his own grief in order to care for the children."

"Can't be easy." Lucy tsked. "How are they doing now?"

"If by they you mean the General and the little guests," Poppy walked into the kitchen carrying empty glasses, "Gavin is clobbering him at Old Maid."

"Before that, the General grumbled about losing at War." Cindy followed her sister into the kitchen. "The traditional game of Whist has been put aside until bedtime."

Poppy smiled. "Right now the men are at one table and the ladies at the other. Emily seems to be doing pretty well herself, but I think Nadine is having a hot streak."

"I was thinking," Grams dried her hands on a nearby towel, "up in the attic there are some of the easels you girls used as children. I bet the children would like it if Eric set them up a little paint studio while they're visiting."

"Maybe we can get Eric to paint as well. Isn't it supposed to be good therapy?" Poppy suggested.

"May not help, but it can't hurt." Grams smiled.

From the other room a diminutive voice shouted "Go fish!"

"I guess they've moved on." Iris strained to hear the conversation in the parlor.

"From here, it all sounds so normal. I wouldn't know they'd lost both their parents suddenly." Poppy reached for one of the massive aprons that Lucy always kept by the back door. "Gavin is still a little quiet, but somehow they don't seem so… lost."

"Don't let a little temporary shift fool you." Iris heaved out a heavy sigh. "It's going to be a while before they adjust to whatever their new norm is."

Poppy nodded and yanking the apron tie tight, waved at her cousin. "You'd better get in there and join the game. Emily is waiting for you."

"On my way." Iris spun around and hurried into the parlor where the evening crowd were now playing childhood games. From the way Nadine threw her arms in the air after dropping her cards on the table, anyone would think this was a fierce game of Poker rather than a friendly game of Go Fish.

"Oh, good." Nadine pushed away from the table. "My luck seems to have turned. This young lady is cleaning our clocks. You can have my seat. I'll see about another pot of coffee."

A roar of laughter erupted from the men's table. "You win again," the General said loudly.

Gavin's head bobbed quickly, but there was no accompanying smile. Iris understood that patience, routine, and time was key in this situation, but she couldn't help but wish for a sweet smile. At least he was engaged.

"So," Iris rubbed her hands together, "what are we playing?"

Emily held up a playing card. "Old Maid."

"Old Maid it is." Iris hadn't played the game in many years. Five hands later, she'd yet to win, but didn't care. She'd forgotten how much she enjoyed young children before money and privilege turned them into entitled teens and clueless adults. Every so often she caught Emily smiling. Not very big, and not very long, but a smile, and that was a good thing.

By the sixth round, Eric had stood from the table. "Sorry folks, but it's past bedtime."

Without a word, Emily set the cards on the table and shoved her seat back. For years Iris had been slowly losing patience with the constant attitude of spoiled teens. Whether it was over homework, technology time, or even bedtime, enough was enough. Except right now she'd pay big bucks to get even a trickle of an argument from either of the two children.

His cheetah tucked under one arm, Gavin reached for the deck of cards.

"You planning on playing cards in bed?" Eric's question had been more of a tease.

Little Gavin gripped tightly on the deck and shook his head.

"That's fine if he wants to take the cards home with him." Grams came over and kissed the boy on his head. "Tomorrow we're going to go rock hunting."

Gavin's head lifted high. Iris could see the questions in his eyes. And she had a few as well.

"Rock hunting?" Emily came to stand beside the older woman.

"That's right. We're going to go looking for some pretty flat rocks and then we are going to do some painting."

For a short minute, Iris could see the twinkle in both children's eyes. Maybe she should have brought her Grams to work with her all these years.

CHAPTER SEVEN

"Hi Gil." Eric stepped outside of the cabin to take the call. "I've been trying to get a hold of you for twelve hours. When did you stop checking your messages?" Eric had worked with Gil for close to a decade. He knew as well as anybody that Eric always answered his phone.

"My fault. The lake where we're staying has spotty reception at best."

"Lake?

"Long story. What's up?"

"Persian Gulf. Should have had you wheels up last night."

Eric shook his head even though no one could see. "No can do. I told you I've got my sister's kids."

"Yes, and I am sorry, but there is such a thing as babysitters. Or nannies."

Yeah, he'd certainly come to learn about nannies.

"I would have called Kurt, but the powers that be have specifically asked for you."

"Well, you're going to have to disappoint them. I simply cannot leave now."

"We're ready." Emily appeared on the doorstep, Gavin on her heels.

"Sorry, Gil. Gotta go." Heaving a deep sigh, Eric looked up the hill to Hart House. He wasn't totally sure if it was the company, the location, the food or the people that had his niece and nephew eager for breakfast, but his gut said it was all about the people. Something he was unwilling to risk for any job.

Speaking of special people, by the time they'd closed the cabin door behind them, Lucy was already on the porch waving at the children. "Why, don't you look all spiffied up and ready for your day of rock hunting."

Fiona Hart appeared on the porch beside the family housekeeper, her gaze lifted to the bright blue sky. "It's going to be a wonderful day."

"I do agree, ma'am." Eric nodded at his hostess. "We are all looking forward to today's project."

The momentary flicker of a smile on Emily and Gavin's faces was all Eric needed to know Iris approached the house. Last night, the only thing they had asked for at bedtime was a story from Iris. He had a feeling two nights in a row made her bedtime stories officially part of the steady routine that she'd successfully drummed into him was so important. What he wasn't sure of, was how deeply everything else about Hart Land would be ingrained in the children's ever important routine.

"I want a round rock." Emily stabbed at her pancakes.

Fiona Hart smiled at the child. Tall and thin with silver hair cut sleek just above her shoulders, the woman did not look anything like a typical grandmother. Yet the twinkle in her eye, as bright as the smile on her lips, at the prospect of spending time with two little children, made him think of over-the-river, through-the-woods, and just about anything else about apple pie and doting grandmothers.

"I don't know about any of you," Iris swallowed her last bite, "but I'm so excited to learn something new with my grandmother."

Eric was also excited to learn from Fiona Hart, though he doubted it had anything to do with rocks or painting.

Fiona Hart slapped her hands together. "In that case, let's get hunting."

"Take my Jeep." The General tossed his keys to Iris. "You'll be able to get further up the mountain than with regular car."

Iris merely nodded and caught the keys midair. Within minutes the children had climbed into the car and fastened their seatbelts.

"Miss Fiona," Lucy came hurrying down the steps of the big old house, "I think you'd better take this call. I can't make out which reservation he's talking about. Anything you can do to calm the man down before he blows a gasket would be great."

Fiona turned to her granddaughter. "You guys better go on ahead. I'll be ready when you get back."

For an instant Eric expected the children to somehow protest, but standing on either side of Iris, each child holding a hand, all seemed unscathed.

"Well," Iris said with more enthusiasm than was probably required, "looks like we're on our own. Ready?" Both heads nodded and Iris looked to him.

"Yes, ma'am." He clicked his heels and saluted.

Iris snapped straight. "Don't tell me you're former military? Or has a couple of days with my grandfather turned you into a recruit?"

"Six years with Uncle Sam's Navy. Dad was an electrician, but my grandpop on my mom's side came from a long line of navy men. I suspect the ocean is in our blood."

"So that's why you came to the lake?" She started walking up the hill, away from the water and from Hart House.

Following her direction, he fell in step beside Gavin. "Partly. Though, frankly I don't know that I ever would have found this place on my own. My sister's uber efficient lawyer must have arranged for Adele's mail to be forwarded to me before sunset the day she died." Part of him meant the statement in jest, but another part realized that pretty much had to be the case for all of this to have come together so fast. "A postcard from the General confirming the family's reservation was in my mail the day after the therapist appointment."

Brows buckled in thought, Iris tilted her head at him. "I suppose that must be part of the General's new marketing strategy. It's been almost a year now since he discovered the joys of the internet."

"Only a year?"

"Well, I'm sure he's used email and other technology, but last year he went to a class reunion and came home with renewed enthusiasm for all things digital. Now he chats online with old friends and plots away new marketing strategies for the cabins."

"I see." The path they followed had narrowed to where Iris led the way with Emily behind her, Gavin and Eric bringing up the rear.

"Just ahead the brook is wider and lower. We can find lots of fun river rocks there." Emily slowed her step and tugged at Iris's arm. It took a few seconds for Iris to recognize what had caught the child's attention. "Oh, those are pretty."

Eric followed the direction the two stared at. A patch of small pink flowers bloomed under a thick stretch of trees. Funny how everything here on Hart Land seemed extraordinary. Even in the thick of the shade, pretty flowers grew.

"Can we pick some for Miss Fiona?" Emily asked.

"You know," Iris smiled at the girl, "I think she'd love that."

Gavin's brow crinkled and his lower lip quivered. "Mama said we shouldn't pick flowers from the park."

"That's right." Iris squat down beside the little boy and pulled him into the circle of her arm. "But we're not in a park."

Without thought, Eric stepped into his niece's side where Iris had inched away, and slipped an arm around her shoulder. Emily's weight leaning against him caught him momentarily off guard. Not the actual weight, but the swelling in his chest at the understanding that this young child trusted him even a fraction more than she had only a few short days ago. The feeling was unexpected, and very new to him, but there was one thing he was very sure of. No matter how incompetent he was, he would not let his sister down.

"Won't they die?" Gavin asked, his lip more shaky.

Iris glanced briefly up at Eric. He certainly hoped she wasn't expecting him to have an answer for the child. That such a young boy made the connection with picking flowers and death was a surprise to him. No way he knew how to answer.

"I bet if we put them in a vase with water as soon as we get home, they'll stay fresh and pretty for everyone to see and enjoy."

Gavin seemed to consider the suggestion with much more intent than Eric would have expected. Finally, he looked to Eric then Iris. "Can we give Mama and Papa a glass of water, wherever they are?"

This time, Eric saw Iris blink back a watery tear and he was guiltily pleased the child had addressed her and not him. What the heck was he supposed to say to that? Without a plan or words, Iris and he switched places. She stood and looped her arm around Emily and he squatted at eye level in front of Gavin. "I bet your mom and dad have all the water they need to drink. I'm also going to bet that right now they're looking down at you and are so proud you remembered not to pick flowers in a park." He thought fast and grasping at straws, tried for redirection. "I also bet they're just waiting to see what you and Miss Fiona do with the river rocks."

Gavin seemed to follow the train of thought more easily and without a word, moved to where his sister and Iris stood side by side.

He raised his hand to Iris, a silent signal it was time to get the rocks. The flowers would have to wait till the walk home. Whoever had told him that things would get easier with time didn't have a blessed clue of what they were talking about. What was his sister thinking leaving these kids to him?

•　•　•　•

"That is an absolutely beautiful rock." Despite the supportive words, Eric didn't look all that convinced.

Their long morning walk yielded a surprisingly large collection of flat rocks, round rocks, shiny rocks and just about any other size or shape imaginable. When Emily and Gavin walked into Hart House, Grams had already set up two child size easels beside her own supplies for the children to use. The rest of the morning had been spent dabbling in colors, shades, mixing, sketching, and of course painting. In some cases, there seemed to be more paint on the kids than the rocks or even the paper Grams had them try their design ideas on, but the kids were having a blast. And frankly, so was Iris.

"Who knew painting rocks could be this entertaining?" Eric leaned into Iris. Grams had set up a place for them to participate. At first the plan had been to only spend a few minutes and let Grams have her fun, but she and Eric got sucked in as well. Now whatever her new job might be, she had plenty of paperweights and doorstops to go with it. As did everyone else.

"What does it say about a man when his four-year-old nephew paints a better daisy then he does?"

"Maybe daisies aren't your thing." Iris smiled. "What else did you try?"

Eric gave a half-hearted shrug and chuckled. "Let's just say, my starfish wasn't any better than my daisy."

"I'm in no better position to judge." Laughing, Iris held up her most recent attempt at a green bullfrog on a lily pad. From the way Eric's face contorted, he wasn't having any easier time seeing the frog then she was. Maybe she should just tell everybody it's a pea in a pod.

All the rocks set aside to dry, Grams walked the children, and the adults, through the steps of cleaning up the brushes and putting away the unused supplies. Iris could tell by the way the children moved, hurrying from task to task, that they were having just as much fun at this part of the process as they'd had with the actual artwork. A glint of pride shown in their eyes whenever they handled the still wet stones. That made Iris want to smile like she hadn't smiled in a long time. Maybe working with children was still an option, just not the spoiled tweens.

Lucy came by carrying two plated dishes. "Aren't we a fine group of artists." She plopped the plates down in front of each child. "If you eat all your lunch, I have some of Lily's Christmas Spitzbuben cookies!"

"But it's not Christmas. Is it?" Gavin swirled his head toward Iris

"No." Lucy ruffled his hair. "It's just a name. The cookies can be made any time of year you want."

The little boy nodded his delight and reached for the cut up sandwich.

"While we've been painting away," Grams slid the drying brushes into a standing container, "the sun has come out full force."

"I actually opened the windows. It's so warm," Lucy called from the doorway on route back to the kitchen.

"I know Mother Nature is merely teasing us, but it seems a shame to let such a beautiful day go to waste."

Iris had to agree with her grandmother on that point at least. But what to do on such a lovely day.

"Your grandfather just had a fresh load of sand dumped down by the lake. You kids used to love helping."

Memories of climbing on the mountains of sand—okay, maybe they were little hills, but to the Hart granddaughters they might as well have been Mount Everest—came rushing back.

"Why don't you two go check out the shore, see what you think? I'll have Lucy pack the desserts and if you think it's a good idea you can eat by the water."

Eric's gaze shifted quickly from her grandmother to the children, back to Grams, out the window to the water and back to the kids.

"I promised Emily I'd teach her to play Jacks. This will be the perfect time. Don't you worry. They'll be fine," Grams encouraged.

Of course Iris knew that, but she suspected part of Eric's hesitation was that he knew that too. Insecurity still bounced off him in waves. He had better instincts than he realized. A bit lacking in the practical, but good instincts. Now she just needed to help him see that. But how?

• • • •

"What are you thinking?" Lucy asked Fiona.

From her spot at the kitchen counter packing up some of Lily's leftover desserts, Fiona kept an eye on the two kids whispering among themselves and slowly devouring the lunch Lucy had made. "That the kids are doing better but have such a long way to go."

"So much sadness in their little worlds." Lucy piled on twice the deli meats in the adult sandwiches.

"It was so nice to see Gerald's granddaughter and her family last year. To see her coming back to her roots." Fiona shook her head. "I'm glad her brother is going to be doing the same."

"We'll see." Lucy sliced the two sandwiches on the diagonal.

Fiona laughed. Never in the middle, that would be sacrilege.

"I'm a bit concerned about that young man," Lucy continued. "He seems a tad overwhelmed. What he needs is a good woman to help him."

"Lucy…"

"Mabel's daughter is still looking. With our Violet falling for Grant, Martha is still in the market for a nice city boy."

"Lucy…" Fiona cautioned again.

"Don't look at me that way. With Martha being the oldest of all those siblings, she's got a good handle on little children."

"Lucy!" Fiona said so sternly that Lucy's brows shot up high on her forehead and her cutting hands stilled. "Not now."

"But there's never a bad time for love."

"Lucy. For me. Please, let's give this man some room before you thrust an unsuspecting wife on him. Okay?"

The woman heaved out a heavy sigh and slowly nodded her head. "I suppose waiting a little bit won't hurt. Besides, the new organist at church might be a good fit too. We'll have to invite her to tea and see."

"Yes, let's wait and do that." Fiona smiled and closed the lid on the dessert box. At least Fiona was sure of one thing. Waitress or organist, Eric Johnson would make a nice catch.

CHAPTER EIGHT

Eric sucked in a deep breath. Fiona had been correct. The early spring chill that had filled the air while they had been off hunting rocks had given way to the heat of a sunny afternoon. Not the kind of heat he'd find if he lived with his grandfather in Florida, but by New England standards this was almost an early summer day.

"Days like this make you want to take your shoes off and dip your toes in the water." Iris tipped her head back and lifted her face to the sun.

For a moment, Eric indulged in studying the woman before him. Long sandy blonde hair down her back, a hint of a suntan contrasted rosy cheeks, and with her eyes closed, long lashes paid homage to the sun. She fit in perfectly with the beauty of Mother Nature. Taking in a deep breath, she opened her eyes and retreated a step.

Not wanting to get caught ogling, he shifted his gaze up toward the house before looking back to the water. "Decided against testing the waters?"

"Oh, no way." She barked out a loud laugh. "The sunshine may be tempting, but anybody raised on this lake knows there's ice water on that shore. Thank you, but I'll wait till July, maybe August."

Eric bit back a muffled laugh. "That late in the summer?"

"I may be New England born and bred, but my blood thinks it has Caribbean roots."

That made him smile. "I know what you mean. My grandfather lives in Florida. The waters are warm enough, but it still doesn't compare to the warm shores of the islands."

"You know," Iris snapped her fingers, "this gives me an idea. When was the last time you built a sand castle on the beach?"

"Suffice it to say, a while." He glanced at the mounds of sand piled near the stone wall. "Someone's gonna have to get at least a little wet to get water to pack the sand."

Iris nodded. "Chicken?"

"Is that a dare?"

Already big blue eyes rounded even larger. "Now would I do that?"

The natural beauty he'd observed just a few moments ago gave way to an impish grin and the twinkle in her eyes that made him take a single step away from the water. When she burst out laughing, he knew she had indeed been thinking exactly what he thought. Only his highly tuned instincts saved him from being toppled into the cold lake waters by a feisty nanny.

"Six years in the Navy." He grinned back at her. "You'll have to do better than that if you want to catch me off guard."

Iris grinned back at him, those wide baby blues brimming with feigned innocence. The sound of pounding feet and chattering children broke the sense that they were the only two people on the lake.

"Miss Fiona said it was okay to come meet you at the water." Emily pointed up the hill to Hart House. From the porch, Fiona Hart could be seen waving back.

"That is an important rule here at the lake." Iris leveled her gaze on the two siblings. "You have to have an adult with you. There's no coming to the water alone."

The simple rule gave Eric his first teaching moment that didn't leave him feeling like the proverbial fish out of water. Squatting in front of his two charges, he reached forward and took hold of each child's hand. "That's an important rule for being in the water everywhere, not just here at the lake. You always go in the water with a buddy. Never go in the water alone."

From the corner of his eye he could see Iris nodding her approval. The recognition gave him an odd kick in the chest. What was that all about?

Shaking away the thought, he and the kids inspected the sand piles while Iris hurried up to the house to retrieve the necessary equipment for sand construction. She must have known exactly where her grandmother stored the goods because in a very short time she was hurrying down the path waving shovels and buckets and a bag of cups at them.

The first attempt at a foundational tower fell apart in front of him.

Practically rolling her eyes at him, Emily shook her head. "That's not how you do it. You have to pack the sand really tight and just a little wet."

For a six year old, Emily seemed to have the art of sand castle making down pat. A few efforts later and with a nod of approval from his niece, Eric reached for a large plastic cup and packed it full of sand to stack on top of the makings of a tower worthy of Rapunzel and her golden hair. He'd forgotten just how much fun playing on the beach could be. So used to being by the water only for work, he'd forgotten the simple joys of building a makeshift castle.

"That's very good, Uncle Eric." Emily almost smiled at him.

The words thank you barely made it past the lump in his throat and through his lips. This was the first time she'd mentioned him by name. Somehow, hearing her say Uncle Eric today felt way more important than when she'd muttered Uncle Eric the last time he'd seen her. Had it really been almost two years since that awkward Thanksgiving at his grandfather's?

"Now you have to put little dents around the edge to make it look like a real castle," Emily instructed without looking up from her construction.

Gavin paused from working on the moat with Iris, shovel in hand, and glanced over at Eric. "That's the way Daddy does it."

It took a few seconds for Gavin to realize he'd spoke of his father, and then another second to realize Daddy wasn't here in the present anymore.

Before a sad moment washed away the fun they'd been having, Iris poured a half cup of water into the partially constructed moat. "Who was in charge of moats?"

"Me!" Emily shouted. "But Uncle Eric needs my help with the towers."

Gavin hesitated, looked down at his shovel and then up at Emily again. "So I'm the new moat maker?"

A relieved breath of air swooshed out of Eric's lungs. He didn't know what the little boy was feeling or even thinking, but he'd happily chalk one up for distraction and a saved day. Now he only had another fourteen or so years to get through. How the heck was he going to manage?

• • • •

"I promise, if you come back in the summer we'll bury someone in the sand." Iris held the screen door open for the children. The sand castle had turned into an entire compound and it was a total and complete success, even if perhaps the castle was tilted slightly to the left. What Iris had not anticipated, nor had Eric, was that the sandcastle building tradition in his sister's family had ended with burying their father in the sand. Somehow that image simply didn't jive with the picture Eric had painted of the stuffy Englishman.

"Can we come back in the summertime?" Gavin asked.

Surprise flashed in Eric's eyes. Whether it was at the question of them coming back together or whether it was that he didn't have an answer, she didn't know. "Maybe," he answered. Her money was on he didn't have a clue.

Gavin nodded. "Will tomorrow be summer yet?"

Somehow Eric's eyes grew even wider, and Iris had to smother a smile. Clearly the man had no idea the kind of questions children could come up with, or their lack of concept of time. Any parent who had ever ridden in a car with their young children on a road trip, and fended off the every five-minute question of "are we there yet," understood his current dilemma. "No, sport." Eric shook his head. "Summer is still a long time away."

The munchkin was still peppering Eric with questions about the upcoming summer, and distance, and time, and possibly the rudimentary elements of the universe when they met up with Grams sitting by a window inside, easel set up, paintbrush in hand, and who knew what on the canvas. "If you wash your hands good and clean, I bet Lucy has a treat for you in the kitchen."

Before anybody could say a word the two children nodded, beamed up at the older woman, and spinning on their heels, took off running for the washroom tucked under the grand staircase.

Grams smiled after the two small children. "It really has been too long since we've had small children in this house. It's a nice change."

Phone buzzing in his pocket, Eric looked down at the number, and let out a soft sigh before answering. "No."

Even though the phone was not on speaker, Iris could still hear the response. "Don't you want to hear what I have to say?"

"No."

"Kurt can't go either. He's getting over an ear infection."

"Sorry, man. I can't go now. It's not happening. What about Jim?"

"Are you really going to make me call him?"

"Yes. I am."

"You do realize if he goes out there, there's a really good chance we'll need you to go back and fix it anyhow?"

"A risk I'm willing to take."

Iris could hear the man's groan on the other end of the phone loud and clear. "All right. I'll call Jim." The guy didn't even bother with goodbye, the call simply disconnected.

Setting her paint pallet to one side, Grams looked up at him. "Problems?"

"Not really." Eric shook his head.

Grams raised one eyebrow and stared at him in warm, patient silence.

"Well, maybe a little. I have a very specialized job, and I don't work 9 to 5 like most people. I designed a specialized deep water drill mechanism. Whenever there's a problem, I'm one of only a handful of people qualified to repair it. And I get paid very well to stop at the drop of a hat and go where I'm needed. By the time another repair is needed, Kurt will be over his infection and able to handle it. I'm not sure when I'll be able to do that again, but the near immediate future won't be it."

"A lot of single parents find ways to make difficult jobs work." Grams waved a hand at Iris. "My granddaughter has been practically raising other people's children for years."

"I'm not sure I like the sound of that." Mostly because Iris wasn't very fond of how the children had turned out. Rich helicopter parents with a bad habit of substituting money and objects for quality parenting time easily trumped her best efforts.

Eric's brows buckled in thought. "I guess a nanny wouldn't be a bad idea."

"Don't look at me." Iris waved her hands the way an umpire would for a runner safe at base. "It's time to put my psych degree to better use." Though heaven knows what job that would be. After all these years she found herself right back where she'd been after graduating college—facing years of post grad studies if she wanted to put her degree to work. Only then, when a chance to fill in for a wayward nanny for one of her parents' friends fell in her lap, she'd jumped at the opportunity. The problem now was the same as back then, she had little interest in going back to school. Besides, at this point if she were a licensed counselor of any kind, she'd be more inclined to tell people to suck it up than to help them work out their issues.

"No," Eric said. "I just mean that unless I plan on changing careers at this point—which since I like my job, I'd rather not—I am going to need someone I can trust to care for the children from time to time." He heaved another slightly deeper sigh.

Something in the press of his lips told Iris he didn't like that idea any better than she did. And why should it bother her, they weren't her children.

CHAPTER NINE

So many things tumbled around inside Eric's head. He'd had the children little more than a week, most of which was a blur. For the first time in his life he understood what the expression a fish out of water meant. In less than 24 hours, he'd received a phone call from an attorney—no, a solicitor—in London, learned of the fatal accident, and picked up two very quiet unaccompanied minors from the airport. From that moment on he'd been treading water.

If only his sister hadn't objected to having one of those stuffy British nannies the way her husband had been raised. At least then there would be somebody more capable than him right now making decisions. Of course, his gaze shifted to Iris and the General playing Go Fish with his niece and nephew. At least for now, maybe he did have that.

"You, young man, will either be a brilliant mathematician or an outstanding card shark." The General's words carried more pride then censure. Unlike his first nights at Hart House, tonight was a quiet evening with only the General, Mrs. Hart, Iris and the occasional appearance by Lucy bringing more food or drink.

Walking past the card table, Lucy retrieved Gavin's empty dish of cookies. "My goodness, you are a bottomless pit for those cookies, aren't you?"

Funny, he hadn't, until now, noticed Gavin's voracious interest in the evening snacks. His sister's plate still had three cookies. It looked like they might have to work on curtailing the boys' sweet tooth. Perhaps Iris could help. But now would not be the time. Definitely not yet. Eric just needed to pay more attention to the young boy's diet before turning to comfort foods transformed the kid into a roly-poly.

"It will work out." Fiona Hart flashed him a quick reassuring smile before returning her attention to the sketchpad in her lap. She must have given up on the painting she'd been working on before supper. Or perhaps she just wanted a change of pace. Though he suspected she needed practice anyway. While this afternoon's painting had a lovely array of colors, he didn't have a clue what the picture was supposed to be. Apparently she was much better at offering reassurance and sound advice than at watercolors.

Casually, the older woman glanced at her wristwatch. The subtle movement reminded Eric that he needed to be on alert for bed time. According to his own timepiece, the kids should have been getting ready for bed almost thirty minutes ago. Blast. When was he going to get the hang of this?

"This will have to be the last round. It's time for bed," he announced with as much self-confidence as he could muster. Too bad he didn't feel as sure as he hoped he sounded.

"Is Miss Iris going to read to us again tonight?" Gavin asked.

Unlike previous nights, this time Iris didn't hesitate. "Absolutely." He hoped that meant she was getting as comfortable with the children as they were with her.

Within minutes, the last game was over and Iris was the first to push away from the table. Clutching his favorite little stuffed cheetah backpack to his side, Gavin fell in step beside her. His sister at Iris's other side.

"Guess we're all set." Iris smiled down at her two shadows.

The sound of the screen door squeaking open had everyone looking up. Her hair in a long braid down her back, and sporting a flowing colorful skirt that made her look as much an artist as her grandmother, Poppy strode inside shaking her head and smiling. "I was all set to settle in with my new book and a hot cup of tea only to discover somehow we managed to run out of milk."

"Help yourself, sweetie." Fiona Hart smiled at her granddaughter. Tilting her head, observing her handiwork from a new angle, for a second Eric got the impression she couldn't make out what she was drawing either.

Poppy had made it only a few steps when she caught up with Gavin and Emily. Squatting down, she patted the top of the stuffed animal's head. "This fellow seems to be a good friend. What's your leopard's name?"

Tightening his grip on the plush feline, Gavin mumbled,

"Cheetah."

"That's a nice name." Poppy pushed to her feet, tussled Gavin's curly hair, and pausing to kiss her grandmother on the cheek, continued on her way to the kitchen.

It struck him suddenly that in all these days, it had never occurred to him to ask his nephew if the stuffed animal he kept close at hand had a name. Though he wasn't completely sure if Gavin was sharing the name, or correcting Poppy's assumption—much like his—that the cheetah was a leopard. Either way, what kind of uncle did that make him?

"You ready?" Iris asked softly, moving to stand beside him.

He nodded, ushering her and the kids through the door and waving at his hosts. "Thanks again. We'll see you tomorrow."

"If we get into our pajamas extra fast, can we get two stories?" Emily asked. Other than that first day, there'd been no more complaints about different cabins or colored doors.

Iris hesitated and slipping the key into the door, Eric realized it was his place to say something, but what? He certainly didn't want to impose on Iris, and he had no idea if a second story was a good or bad idea. Shoving the door, he held it open, glanced at Iris, and letting the children walk under his arm into the house, raised a questioning brow at her, coupled with a now-what shrug.

"If it's all right with your uncle," she followed them in, "it's fine with me."

That was all the encouragement the children needed. Fortunately for them, he had no intention of objecting. In a flash they took off across the room and had brushed their teeth, changed their clothes and climbed into bed, awaiting their stories. Oddly enough, he found himself equally eager to hear Iris sharing the latest escapades of Nancy Drew. And what did that say about him?

• • • •

"Fearful that Nancy and Ned were trapped, Bess cried their names in terror." Iris glanced at her audience. Finding them both soundly asleep, she closed the book.

"You can't stop now," Eric said too sincerely. "You have to be near the end."

"I am," she confirmed. "And I'm only reading it once so the rest will have to wait until they are very wide awake again."

Eric's face crumpled much like a pouting child before the deep lines soothed and he blew out a resigned huff. "Could I interest you in a cup of tea or hot chocolate?"

"Mm, that would be nice. It's been a busy day."

"It has." He crossed the short distance to the kitchen cupboards. "And I have this terrible feeling that it's only going to get worse."

"You're probably right." She slid onto a stool and faced him. "That's the way parenting works. As soon as you figure out the rules, someone changes them all."

"Could be, but I'm not their parent." He slid the teapot under the running water and sucking in a hiss, he turned to face her. "Though I guess now I am, aren't I?"

All she could bring herself to do was force a sympathetic smile and nod at him. She didn't have the heart to tell him that even though circumstances made this time in the children's lives unbearably difficult, these were probably the easiest years he'd have ahead of him. "Do you have any plans for tomorrow?"

"None." The kettle whistled and he turned off the stovetop flame. "Although…"

"Yes?"

"Tomorrow is supposed to be another warm day. I wonder if the kids have ever been fishing."

She hadn't seen that coming, but the way he had eyed that rod at the One Stop, it shouldn't have been such a surprise to her. "There's only one way to find out."

"My grandfather took me fishing when I was a little boy. Probably not much older than Gavin." He set a cup of hot water and teabag in front of her, then nudging the sugar bowl closer, slid into the seat beside her. "You would think that sitting in a canoe at the crack of dawn in total silence would not be something a little boy would enjoy, but the anticipation of getting that nibble on the end of the line was better than awesome."

"I can see in your eyes how sweet the memories are."

"Honestly, I have to admit, getting to put a fresh worm on a hook was a big part of the fun too."

"Oh, I bet." She didn't bother to smother a laugh. She knew little boys too well.

"And of course, after we'd caught our limit—or at least what I thought was our limit—we'd get to dive in and do a little swimming."

"Sounds like a lot of good fun. The General always talked of going fishing, but I don't know that he ever did. Maybe if he'd had grandsons."

"Wouldn't have made a difference. My sister was champion worm digger."

"That would have been Cindy. Lack of aversion to worms probably comes with the territory of being a veterinarian. Especially one with hopes of building a wild life refuge. That requires a tolerance for all of God's creatures, large or small or squirmy."

"Wild life refuge?"

Iris nodded. "She does all she can for critters regardless of whether or not they're domesticated, but she's right that the mountain needs something bigger than just her and her little clinic. Rehabbing wild life, especially to return to the wild, requires a lot more time and facility space than she has available."

"Sounds like a worthy cause."

"Yeah." Somehow she felt like she was the only cousin to have grown up without one. Heather was working on the new wing for the nearest hospital, Violet was on a one woman mission to bring inner peace to the universe, Lily singlehandedly contributed to the gastronomic delight of most residents and guests within a fifty mile radius, of course Cindy had her refuge, Callie was encouraging fair play among the country's youth—not an easy task with high schoolers. In an off-handed way, Poppy contributed to the spiritual well-being of the community. After all, keeping the books could be considered fundamental in keeping the church—and hence, the community—afloat. That left Zinnia, who would probably some day take over the winery and keep the state of New York, as well as most of the East Coast, in heart healthy red wine.

"Did I say something wrong?" A deep V formed at the bridge of his nose.

She'd been seriously lost in her own thoughts. "What?"

"You're frowning," he supplied.

"Oh. Sorry. Every time I consider what am I going to do with my life now, I probably look like I sucked on a rotten egg."

"Ick." His whole face crumpled. "That is a nasty visual."

"Sorry," she repeated.

"And staying in the nanny business is out of the question?"

"Completely. I'm done with other people's children." She thought she heard a slight wince and realized how that must have sounded. "Sorry."

"You say that a lot."

"Lately, yes."

"And that has something to do with why you need to put your degree to a new use?"

She shrugged. "Maybe a little, but mostly, I simply grew tired of the teenage battleground. I should probably get up close and personal with the classifieds. A new job isn't going to waltz up to Hart House and jump into my lap."

"You never know." His forehead creased in deep thought again.

"What has you doing such a wonderful Shar Pei impression?"

Pushing to his feet, he carried his empty cup to the sink. "Would you like some more?"

"No thank you." She shifted on the stool. "Why so serious again?"

"Thinking too much."

"What about now?"

The dishes clanked in the deep stainless sink. "Talking about your job got me thinking about mine. Usually, I have a pretty strict workout regimen. My job requires I be in top condition at the drop of a hat. I've been neglectful since taking charge of the kids."

"Yes, I can imagine. If I can help in any way." Had she really said that. Where had her mouth missed the memo about not wanting to work with kids anymore? Though this wasn't work exactly. Emily and Gavin reminded her of why she'd become a nanny. Maybe looking for a new line of work could wait a little longer. At least until Emily and Gavin were home once again. After all, what harm could an extended leave of absence do? Especially if she got to spend that time quietly sipping tea with good company.

Oh, who was she trying to kid? Spending all this time with one good looking struggling uncle was as appealing as any new job she might find. Yes, she felt sorry for the guy, but it turned out he seemed to have some pretty decent instincts, he cared, and he was trying. In her book that made him one of the keepers. Keeper? Oh man, what in heaven's name was she thinking?

CHAPTER TEN

"**L**ovely day for a walk around the lake." Retired General Harold Hart slathered cream cheese on his bagel. "I must admit, my bones would not complain if Mother Nature gave us the gift of early summer this year."

Briefly this morning, Eric had considered making breakfast for the kids instead of joining the family, but he'd quickly reconsidered how much they—Emily especially—enjoyed eating breakfast beside Fiona Hart. Truth be told, he enjoyed chatting with the General as well. Listening to the man talk reminded Eric a great deal of his own grandfather, also a military man, and one he didn't visit often enough. He would have to change that. An even better idea now that his grandfather's only two great grandchildren were in Eric's custody.

"I must agree." Fiona nodded at her husband. "Winter was rather harsh to New England this year. An early summer would be a lovely apology from Mother Nature. I may take that walk with you."

"Can't think of anything I'd like better." The General smiled up at his wife and Eric could almost feel the love radiating across the room. Not what he'd expected from a gruff Marine.

"Sorry I'm so late." Iris hurried into the room. "I made the mistake of answering the phone without looking. The Throckmortons have decided this summer will be a good time for a trip to Antarctica and for some inexplicable reason they actually thought I'd jump at the chance to join them."

"Antarctica is a beautiful place." Her grandmother smiled.

"It's cold," Iris stated emphatically while stabbing rather harshly at a couple of pancakes.

"At least they thought enough of you to want you along." Fiona dabbed at the corners of her mouth with her napkin.

"Or they can't find anyone crazy enough to accompany them and their two spoiled offspring on a trip to the opposite end of the earth." She plopped into what had become their regular seats at the table, smiling broadly at each child before taking a long swig of hot coffee.

"Your grandfather was just saying that today is perfect weather for a long walk. Why don't you join us? The fresh air will do wonders for your mood."

"Can we come?" Emily asked. Gavin didn't look terribly convinced that was a good thing.

"Of course you may," Fiona answered. "Everyone is welcome."

"Will Lady and Sarge come too?" Gavin asked the General.

"They wouldn't miss a good walk."

"Okay then." Swinging his feet under his seat, apparently all it took to make something a good idea for Gavin was to add a couple of friendly Golden Retrievers to the mix.

The General turned his attention to Eric. "You in too?"

"Actually, I was just thinking I needed to get more exercise."

"Too bad our Violet isn't around." Fiona tsked. "She'd get you into shape."

"She has more interesting things keeping her in Boston these days," Iris added with a smile.

"Love will do that to you." The General quickly lifted a cup to his mouth, but not before Eric noticed the grin the man tried to hide.

He did his best to smother his own smile. He vaguely remembered that Violet was one of the cousins, but he seriously doubted unless she was a close relative of Arnold Schwarzenegger that she'd do him much good.

"Perhaps you could take a nice run while the rest of us go for a walk," Iris suggested.

"Do you like to jog?" the General asked.

"Normally I run about five miles a day. Lately, well, I haven't been."

The General's eyes opened wide with interest.

"I like to run." Gavin lifted his gaze from his bowl of cereal. "Can I run too? I bet Lady and Sarge like to run." He turned to the General. "Don't they?"

"I don't know about five miles." The General smiled and faced Eric. "But if you're serious, we have some nice hiking trails, but one in particular is gravel and wide enough for my Jeep to fit."

"Jeep?" he asked, unsure of how that fit into the getting more exercise scenario he'd mentioned.

"Yes. You can run the trail and Iris and the kids can follow close behind. Maybe keep time for you or just cheer you on. Like Rocky."

Both Emily and Gavin looked up at the General but it was Emily whose brows buckled in confusion and finally asked, "Rocky?"

"A movie before your time." The General straightened his shoulders and turned to Eric. "Unless you have other plans for the day?"

"As a matter of fact, I had thought it might be nice to spend some time on the lake. That is, if there are any boats available."

"Absolutely. We have paddle boats that the kids all love. A couple of canoes. There's an old bass fishing boat in the main shed, and we have a special arrangement with the marina owner if you'd like to use a speedboat for waterskiing or just riding around. Do the children swim?"

The question grabbed Eric by the throat. He had no idea. As a matter of fact, this was probably one of a great many things he didn't know about his own niece and nephew.

To his relief, Emily had been paying attention and answered for him. "I can swim. Gavin still needs to wear his floaties."

"Mama said that after lessons this summer I wouldn't need them anymore." Gavin returned his focus to the nearly empty cereal bowl. His second helping; it was almost as though the kid was afraid he'd never be fed again.

"He doesn't like swimming underwater," Emily offered. "It took me two summers of lessons to swim underwater, but now everyone says I swim like a fish."

"A beautiful fish," Fiona added, and Emily beamed up at her.

"Speaking of fish." Eric cleared his throat and addressed the children. "Have either of you ever been fishing?"

Shaking his head, Gavin's eyes lit with interest. At the same time, Emily's face contorted almost painfully as she muttered, "Ew."

From the corner of his eye he could see Iris swallowing a laugh. "Maybe it's not that bad."

"I'd rather ride in the Jeep." Emily looked to Fiona. "Or walk with you."

"Maybe," Fiona started, her cheeks pulling back in a smile as she spoke, "it could be fun to give it all a try?"

This time Emily didn't seem so sure. She looked from Fiona to her brother to Iris and over to him then back again.

"Do you like riding in boats?" he asked.

The little girl nodded.

"And cars?"

"I've never been in a Jeep."

He suspected she didn't truly understand what the General's Jeep was, but that was okay. "How about we go for a ride in a boat this morning? We'll take it over to the One Stop and buy some fishing poles from Ms. O'Leary, and if you don't want to fish, you'll at least have a nice ride. Then later today we can see about that ride in a Jeep."

She seemed to consider his words a few minutes, glanced toward Fiona who was nodding slightly, and meekly muttered, "Okay."

Not the start of a bond-building experience he'd hoped for, but at least he knew how to fish.

• • • •

"You're doing what?" Cindy set the dirty dishes she carried down next to the sink.

"Going fishing." Iris still wasn't too sure how she got talked into this one, but it was her or Grams, and before she could answer yay or nay, Grams was off on a walk with the General.

Poppy carried in more dirty dishes from the dining room. "You're not kidding?"

"How different can it be from riding on the lake or going waterskiing?" Iris grabbed one of the oversized aprons hanging on the wall. "I'll sit on the boat, encourage the children, and if push comes to shove, I'll help drop a fish in the basket or cooler or whatever it is they keep them in."

Poppy and Cindy glanced at each other. Iris wasn't sure who had the bigger smirk.

"Oh, for heaven sakes," Lucy tied her apron behind her back, "all she has to do is catch them. I'm the one who gets to clean them, debone them, and cook them. I don't see where the problem is."

Shaking her head, she shifted the dirty dishes into sudsy water. "Besides, if you're any good at it, Margaret Benson's oldest son just moved back to Lawford. I understand he's quite the fisherman."

Iris felt all the blood rush from her head to her toes. Matchmaking words from Lucy were grounds for ducking and taking cover at Hart House. The woman had yet to match up two people who actually liked each other, never mind were meant to be together. "I'm sure this is going to be a one time thing, Lucy. I like my fish sautéed in butter with lemon, not on a hook."

Cindy sidled up to her and grabbed the apron out of her hand, then leaned in speaking softly. "I suggest you skedaddle before you give Lucy any more ideas."

"Bless you," Iris whispered back, and with a quick wave goodbye, hurried out of the kitchen praying that when it came to Lucy and matchmaking, out of sight would mean out of mind.

Glancing at her watch, she debated if she needed to change into something a little warmer for being on the lake, or if she should stop at Eric's cabin to see how he was doing getting the kids ready. The decision was made for her when the red door opened.

"We're ready," Emily announced. "Uncle Eric said I can pick out any candy I want at the One Stop to take on the ride."

So apparently the man had discovered the benefits of outright bribery when needing a child to cooperate. "He did, huh?"

Behind Emily's back, Eric shrugged.

Emily's head bobbed. "He says having the right food for the people in the boat is as important as the right food for the fish in the water."

"Makes sense," she answered Emily, but looked to Eric who shrugged again.

Gavin stayed close to his uncle's side, clutching his little backpack to his chest. He seemed to be growing more dependant on the thing rather than needing it less as he adapted to his new surroundings.

"Want me to carry that for you?" she asked.

Instead of handing it over, his grip tightened and his head rattled roughly from side to side. "No."

"No what?" Eric coached from behind.

"No, thank you."

"Good job." Eric patted the boy's shoulder, unaware of Gavin's growing attachment to his Cheetah. Or at least not letting on. "The General arranged with the marina to leave us a boat parked at the One Stop."

"Then we're all set." Taking hold of Emily's hand, she helped load the kids and then herself into the car. A fishing she was going. Who'd have thunk?

In no time at all, they pulled into the parking lot at the One Stop. Eric perused the dock and the sleek red boat tied to it. Nodding his head, he ushered the kids quietly inside.

"Well, now." Katie O'Leary smiled from behind the cash register. "Isn't this a pleasant early morning surprise."

"We thought we'd try our hands at fishing," Eric responded.

"Oh, it's a glorious day for being out on the water. Would you be the one Bobby left the boat at my dock for?"

"We would."

Katie nodded. "Well, you'll be needing plenty of snacks and refreshing drinks. This time of year, the fish are slow to bite. Unless…" She looked over her shoulder as if there had been somebody else in the store who might overhear, and whispered, "Morton's Cove."

If Iris remembered correctly, Morton's Cove was clear across the lake, tucked away from the main boat traffic. "Is that the inlet just past the Carter property?"

"It is. You'll have to turn the motor off and float your way in so you don't scare away the few fish that are around, but if you do you'll have fresh fish for dinner tonight."

"Dinner?" Gavin looked up at Katie. "We have to eat it?"

Smiling, Katie squatted to Gavin's level. "Just like the olden days when strong men hunted for food, fisherman fish for food. Best fish you'll ever eat comes from our lake."

Gavin didn't say a word and Emily's face contorted the same way it had when Eric had first mentioned fishing.

"Of course," Katie continued, "the best part is the homemade ice cream for dessert. It's a rule, you know."

Gavin shook his head. Whether because he didn't know or didn't agree, Iris wasn't sure.

"Yes sir, anyone who has fresh lake fish for dinner gets ice cream for dessert. Extra scoop too."

And with that extra little bribe, both kids were on board. Katie packed a cooler full of fresh juices and snacks, ranging from popcorn to carrot sticks—though Iris was pretty sure the donut holes were going to be very popular—and with new fishing poles and bait in hand, sent them on their way.

If only all of life's challenges could be solved with an extra scoop of ice cream.

CHAPTER ELEVEN

"You look awfully lost in thought this morning." Over the decades, Fiona had learned to read the many moods of her complex husband. This morning's was proving a bit challenging for her. "Is it this month's appointment? Something you don't know how to tell me?"

He smiled and patted the hand tucked into the crook of his elbow. "Nothing like that."

"The girls?"

"Not exactly."

"Ah. Then it has to be the children. So sad."

He nodded. "I know they've not even been here a week, but I had hoped to see some sign of progress."

"Oh, Harold. Even boot camp takes weeks to turn your boys into Marines. You can't fix a broken heart in a few days. Not even our lake can do that."

"I know. But still…"

In so many ways, the General was as much a hopeless romantic as a hard-core Marine. The man wanted everybody to live happily ever after. From the dogs they loved, to the animals Cindy rescued, to their friends and neighbors, their guests, and especially their granddaughters. She could see the light in his eyes brighten as each of their granddaughters found the perfect match. But the heartbreaking situation with Emily and Gavin was clearly weighing heavily on her husband, and this time she didn't have a clue how to make any of it better.

$$\bullet\ \bullet\ \bullet\ \bullet$$

Doing as Katie had suggested, they floated along the cove until Eric found a spot he liked enough to drop anchor. The way he looked about and lifted his nose to the air, it almost looked as though he were a Bloodhound sniffing out the fish. "This looks like as good a spot as any."

"Spot for what?" Emily looked around.

"Fishing."

"Are we really going to have to eat fish?" Gavin asked.

"That depends. A lot of time the fun of fishing is in catching the fish. Often we do what's called catch and release. After they get hooked, we toss them back in the water."

"Why catch them if you're going to give them back?" Emily asked.

A perfectly reasonable question, Eric was especially glad that Emily was involved enough to have asked. The thing was how do you explain to a six-year-old about endorphins or adrenaline? He'd often compared the rush of excitement when the fish takes the bait as the feeling a person gets when they hit a bonus spin on a slot machine. Except his niece and nephew were no more likely to understand gambling than they were the thrill of man against nature.

"The other day, when Mrs. Hart taught you to play jacks?"

Emily nodded.

"How fun was it when you scooped up the jack?"

The corners of her mouth tipped up. "Very."

"And how did you feel when you were able to scoop up more jacks with each bounce of the ball?"

This time her lips tipped upward in a solid smile. "Happy."

"Well," he hefted a lazy shoulder, "it's the same thing. I calculate where to stop the boat, what to put on the hook, just enough tension on the line so I don't lose the fish if he bites, and then when I pull him into the boat, I feel as happy as if I'd picked up a whole bunch of jacks on one bounce."

The explanation seemed to make sense to Emily as her head continued to bob.

"So, the same way you toss the jacks back on the ground to try again, sometimes we toss the fish back in the water to try again."

"But I don't ever eat the jacks." Her nose wrinkled. "I guess that's the big difference."

Eric couldn't help but smile. "Yes. A very big difference."

Based on the crinkled nose, he was pretty sure Emily was not going to want to put the bait on the hook. Carefully doing it for her, he set her rod aside and looked to Iris. She'd been quiet most of the ride and he wondered what she must be thinking. "You want to bait your own hook?"

She took a second to look over the bait and then glanced over the side of the boat. "No, thanks."

"No problem." Prepping her rod, he didn't notice her studying him until he handed it over to her.

"You really enjoy this, don't you?"

"I'd forgotten how much."

"How long has it been since you've been fishing?"

"Too long. I was about six or so when my dad tossed some bagel over the side of the boat and I watched the catfish swim to the surface and gobble it up. Next time we put it on a hook. That's when I caught my first fish. You might say I was hooked."

"Why don't we use bagels?" Gavin asked.

"We could, but this should work better." Now he had Gavin's interest too. So far so good. Not until this moment did he realize just how badly he wanted to be able to relate to them over anything other than the loss of their mom and dad.

"Bagels I might be willing to touch," Iris teased, making him smile.

The woman was amazing, putting her life on hold to help him. Well, she was probably doing it more for the kids than for him, but still, she was smart, thoughtful, kind and damn pretty. What might it take for her to fall for him hook, line, and sinker?

• • • •

For the first time since meeting Eric Johnson, Iris got the feeling she was finally seeing him in his element. The man moved swiftly, with confidence. Not once did she see any signs of doubt, or confusion, or that stunned look that so often appeared on his face at the discovery of some new aspect of childrearing that he knew nothing about. He even seemed to stand a few inches taller. She liked this side of Eric Johnson, and wouldn't mind the chance to get to know the real him a little better.

"All right." He flashed two thumbs up to no one in particular. "I think we're ready to go. Gavin, why don't you let us move your backpack to someplace more protected where it won't get wet?"

No surprise to Iris, the little boy pressed the cheetah backpack more closely to his chest.

"You won't be able to hold the fishing pole if you don't let go of your backpack." Eric reasoned with his nephew.

"Sure I can." Letting go of his grip with one hand, he reached for the nearby pole, accidentally dropping the bag to the floor.

The bag fell closest to Iris. Without thinking, she leaned forward and picked it up, stunned by the weight. "My goodness. What have you got in here?"

The little boy scrambled to reach for the plush backpack but his sister beat him to it, reaching in the bag and knocking a few items onto the floor. Much to Iris's surprise, a stash of cookies from Hart House fell onto the floor of the small boat. After the cookies tumbled one of the rocks they'd painted with Grams and Sarge's sloppy tennis ball.

Emily snatched the pack close before Gavin could get to it.

"Give me that." Gavin lunged toward the cheetah in his sister's hands. "That's mine."

Holding the bag just out of Gavin's reach, Emily stuck her hand inside and pulled out a Berenstein Bears book.

Gavin's lower lip trembled as he stretched closer to the bag and whimpered, "That's mine."

As quiet and sad as they often appeared, this was the first time Iris had seen the near emotional collapse of the two children as they fought a tug-of-war over his precious cheetah.

Eyes wide, Eric spun about to step between the two. "What's this all about?"

"She has my Cheetah." Gavin pointed, failing to hold back the droplets of water pooling in his eyes. "It's mine."

"That's Sarge's ball," Emily countered. "And the painted rocks are supposed to stay at Ms. Fiona's."

Suddenly things were starting to add up and Iris didn't like it. If she didn't miss her mark, Gavin was collecting things that mattered to him. Things he wanted to control. That wouldn't be taken away from him like his mom and dad. Oh hell.

Eric held the bag of cookies in his hand and the crevice at the bridge of his nose deepened. She had the feeling he was coming to the same conclusions she'd just reached. Slowly he lowered himself and leaned back on his heels. "Hey, buddy. Do you want to tell me what this is all about?"

The tone in his voice had lowered softer than Iris had ever heard him speak. Yep, he had definitely figured it out.

Gavin shook his head. "I want my Cheetah."

Extending his arm toward his niece, Eric sucked in a deep breath. "Let me have the bag please."

Emily seemed to think twice about it and Gavin lunged once again in her direction, this time bumping into his sister. Almost toppling her over the side, her grip loosened and the precious Cheetah splashed into the murky water.

"Cheetah!" Gavin cried loudly before falling into a crumpled ball, sobbing uncontrollably.

Steadying Emily on her seat, Eric spun about and scooped Gavin into his arms and carried him in one large step to Iris. "See if you can calm him down. I'll be right back."

All she'd had time to do was wrap her arms around the tearful little boy when Eric kicked off his shoes and dove over the side, taking Iris's breath with him.

Emily leaned over. "Uncle Eric!"

"It's okay," Iris said as calmly as she could manage in her own frenzied state. What the hell was he doing? That water was like ice still. "I'm sure he's going to grab the bag and be up in a minute."

Her words snapped Gavin's head up from her shoulder and even helped slow the sobs to gulping breaths. With the back of his hand the little boy swiped at his watery cheeks, his chest heaving in and out, his eyes fixed on the water.

Everyone's eyes were fixed on the water. How many seconds could the average adult male hold his breath? How long for hypothermia to be a problem? How long had he been under?

Iris said her prayers and fumbled for her phone, all the while staying focused on the small bubbles of air. Until there were none. Oh, hell.

CHAPTER TWELVE

D amn, the water was cold as a polar bear's pool. Unable to see past his fingers, Eric waved his arms, hoping the weighted bag wasn't dropping any faster than he was. Kicking his feet, pushing as deep as he dared, he slashed at the water again.

Bingo. His fingers caught on something soft and he prayed it was his nephew's prized possession. Blowing out his last bit of air, he propelled himself upward until he broke the water line, sucked in a deep breath of fresh air and took a good look at Cheetah dangling from his fingers.

"Oh my God," Iris yelled. "Are you okay?"

"Could be better." Lunging forward, he swam the short distance to Iris and the kids, tossed Cheetah into the boat and levered himself over after it. "The waters of Antarctica might be warmer."

"He's safe. For now. I'm bringing the boat back. We'll need some blankets and hot liquids," Iris said.

Whipping his wet shirt off, it took him a moment to realize Iris was on the phone. "I'm okay. The sun will warm me up."

"The sun isn't that hot," she barked back, rummaging through the bench storage. "They should have blankets in here."

Eric pushed to his feet and crossed to lift anchor. He might not be on death's doorstep, but she was right about one thing, he needed to warm up a helluva lot more than the late spring sun could do for him.

"Where are you going?" She slammed the bench shut and taking a quick glance at the kids, beat him to the anchor. "Sit."

"I can—"

"So can I." She slid out of her lightweight jacket. "It's not much but put this on your shoulders until we get to shore."

He didn't dare say another word. The woman had taken over the situation much like he suspected her grandfather would have. Pulling back on the throttle, she steered the boat away from the cove and across the lake considerably faster than the speed at which they'd arrived. He had to make a considerable effort not to smile at her. The woman was seriously amazing.

"I'm sorry." Emily moved to sit next to him, her expression not one of sorrow that he'd come to see so often, but of concern. For him.

"Me too." Gavin climbed into his lap, apparently not caring at all that from the waist down, Eric was sopping wet.

"Me three."

"You?" Emily asked. "Why?"

"For a lot of things. But for now, let's make a deal." He waited for each of the kids to nod. "If something makes you sad, tell me. If someone or something hurts you, tell me. And from now on, we share everything in this family."

Gavin looked at his soggy Cheetah still lying on the floorboards, climbed out of Eric's lap, picked it up and handed it to him. "I don't think we can eat the cookies now."

"No. I don't think we can."

With a child tucked safely under each arm, Eric blew out a sigh of relief, pleased when Iris looked at him over her shoulder and nodded. Maybe he would get the hang of this yet.

• • • •

"Well, there certainly will be no jogging the trails for you this afternoon." Lucy filled Eric's cup with more warm tea, and walked away muttering, "Diving into the lake."

It was going to take a lot more than Lucy's hot tea or homemade soups for Iris to totally relax. Not even when the elephants in India had scared the bejeezus out of her had her heart rate shot through the ceiling like it had when she saw Eric dive overboard. Even after reaching the shore and being greeted by half the family, including Cole and one of his EMT buddies, just to be sure Eric didn't need to go to the hospital, her nerves were still raw.

"Didn't Lily tell me you're a mechanical engineer?" Cole leaned back in his seat.

Swallowing a sip of tea, Eric nodded. "Yes. That's my degree and training."

"So tell me, how does a pencil pushing, math calculating engineer come out of an ordeal like this almost as if nothing had happened?"

That was what Iris wanted to know.

Eric put the mug of hot tea on the table beside him and loosened the blanket that Lucy kept tightening around his shoulders. "That would probably be because all I do now is make repairs when the tool I designed has a problem."

"The one for deep-sea oil rigs?" the General asked.

Cole leaned forward. "Deep-sea oil rigs?"

"Yep. There are only a handful of divers in the world who can make the repairs."

"Divers?" Iris muttered. As far as she knew, both deep sea diving and oil rig work were dangerous on their own. Combined, the hairs on the back of her neck lifted on end. No wonder the man had not given a second thought to throwing himself overboard. And here she was worried about the cold lake temperatures.

Eric nodded at her. "My career choice keeps me in excellent physical condition. I'm really sorry I scared everybody, but diving in cold water is what I do. So I really could go running this afternoon. It wouldn't be a problem."

"Not happening." The General shook his head. "There are two people in this house who have the last word. My wife Fiona, and Lucy. If they agree you're not going running..."

"I guess I'm not going running." Eric smiled.

Cole held up one hand. "One word of advice. Wear neon colors, avoid the dark early morning hours, and if you hear a motor coming, dive."

"Are you never going to let me live that down?" Lily came through the porch door. "Got here as soon as I heard. So glad everyone is okay. Brought you a little something special."

Eric's eyes tracked the white paper bag Lily held up. The same way he had lifted his chin and sniffed the air when picking a spot to fish, he sniffed the air over the open bag as she set a piece of her mandel bread onto his plate.

"That boring cup of tea will go down much easier if you dunk these in it."

Everyone in the room pushed to their feet reaching for the white bag.

"Ah ah." Lily shook her head. "These are for our guest."

"No fair," Cole almost whined.

Lily reached into the bag and held one up. "What were you telling Eric about jogging on Hart Land?"

"Absolutely nothing." Cole smiled at his fiancée. "Enjoy yourself."

Lily laughed handed him a piece of mandel and kissed him soundly on the lips. "That's the man I love and almost killed."

Everyone in the room laughed along with her. Eric leaned left at Iris. "What am I missing?"

"Long story. I'll tell you later."

Eric nodded, took a bite of the cookie, and swallowed a soft moan. "Outstanding."

"Thank you." Grinning sweetly, Lily sat down next to her fiancé and sidled against him. "How are the children holding up?"

"Pretty well. They're on the veranda with your grandmother painting," Eric replied.

"Frankly," Iris reached for one of the mandels Lily had brought, "I don't think they understood the potential danger. I think they realized he was wet and cold, but they have no idea how dangerous diving into that icy lake can be for the average person." Heaven knows every fear under the sun ran through her mind in what had to be less than a minute.

"That's one of the joys of being a child. Ignorance is bliss." Lucy came back into the room waving a piece of paper. "I forgot in all the commotion to tell you that you got a phone call."

Eric accepted the small sheet of paper, and as he read, pushed to his feet, letting the blanket fall into the chair.

The frown that settled between his brows had Iris pushing quickly to her feet and instinctively moving beside him. "Is something wrong?"

"I don't know. But if you'll excuse me, I think I'm going to take a short walk down by the water."

Hands on her waist, Lucy huffed, preparing to bark orders when the General raised a hand at her palm out, shaking his head.

Something was clearly up. Now the question was should Iris stay put and mind her own business, or follow after him. Technically, she had merely been keeping the family company, helping when she could, nothing more than a casual friend. So why for the second time today was she worried about one Eric Johnson?

• • • •

Roberta. No last name. No discernable information. "We need to talk. Call me when you can" with a phone number he didn't recognize left a great deal to the imagination. An imagination running in all sorts of directions, from someone related to the last repair request he'd turned down, to someone from the children's solicitor's office, to a telemarketer wanting to sell him on a new investment portfolio. Heck, it might even be a dethroned king wanting to share his wealth with Eric.

The moment he broke free of the line of trees, he pulled out his phone. With everything happening of late, since arriving at the lake he'd failed to check voicemails and messages, having answered the few calls that reached him. One number in particular popped up multiple times over the last few days.

"Is there a problem?" Iris stepped off the path onto the sand beside him.

"I don't know." He handed Iris the note. "I'd hoped who ever left the message with Lucy would have left me a more detailed message on voicemail."

"But nothing?"

"Nothing."

Iris handed him back the note and grinned up at him. "Guess there's only one way to find out."

She was right. He could stand here guessing until the next millennium and the only way to get answers was to simply call the number. On the third ring, a digital recording kicked in. Unable to glean any further information from the generic preprogrammed announcement, he left a message of his own and a request for a call back. The last thing he wanted was to play telephone tag, but he'd be the first to admit his curiosity was piqued. He just hoped it didn't turn out to be a telemarketer or a bogus prince. Then again, maybe that would be the easiest scenario. To solve that situation would only require blocking the number and then he could move on with life. "Are you up to a short walk?"

"Always. Especially along the lake."

"You love this place a lot." He took a step forward and waited for her to fall in beside him.

"We all do. There's a special about this place. Almost magical. I don't think anything has changed in over fifty years. There's even a rotary phone on the wall in the kitchen at Hart House."

"Really? That's got to be a hard to find item nowadays."

Iris laughed. The sound seeped into his pores and made him want to laugh too. He really did like being around her. For some insane reason he felt like a teen, itching to hold her hand and if he got lucky, steal a kiss in the moonlight. Except it was broad daylight, he wasn't a teen, and he had more serious things to deal with right now and none of them involved kissing Iris Colby.

"Have you given any thought to something you could do around here?" he asked, shifting to a safer topic of discussion.

Her steps slowed as she turned to look at him. "Funny, I was thinking about that this morning before we met up for breakfast. The obvious thing would be working with children again, but I don't know that I'm up for it anymore."

"You seem to do well enough around Emily and Gavin."

"That's different."

"Why?"

She stopped fully and turned to face him. "Emily and Gavin are sweet kids."

"Don't people say that about a lot of young children? I mean, how many four and six year olds have been tainted by the world?"

Bobbing her head, she picked up the pace, kicking sand behind her. "Don't know that I have an answer, but you're right, it's definitely something worth considering."

It struck him with every passing day that there were a lot of new possibilities worth considering. Especially anything involving Iris Colby.

CHAPTER THIRTEEN

"You just may have a world class baker on your hands." Iris handed Eric another cup of tea. "Sorry, but I promised Lucy."

"My kidneys are probably wondering what has come over me." He set the cup aside on the end table. "Please don't tell me you promised to wrap me in another blanket?"

Iris couldn't help but laugh. "No, but I promised to start a fire."

Poor guy looked like he'd been told someone had run over his new puppy.

"It was that or put you in a guest room at the house so she could hover over you personally. Feeding and fussing over folks is in that woman's DNA." Iris crossed the small living area to the stacked fireplace.

"I'm sorry. I don't mean to be difficult. I know she means well, it's just not that big a deal for me. It's not like we were on the Titanic."

"I know." Pushing to her feet, Iris blew out the match and watched the kindling flare before moving the grill into place and turning to face the man who only a few long hours ago she thought they were going to lose. "You do seem to be fine."

"That's because I am." He reached for the tea cup and brought it to his lips. "Now, tell me about this baker thing?"

"Oh." Iris had almost forgotten. "Emily is having a blast helping Lily bake."

"And Gavin?"

"He seems to just like being with Emily. But she's really paying attention to everything Lily says to her and she's taking it very seriously."

"As seriously as a six year old can."

"Don't underestimate her because of her age. Lily was baking away on her own at eight."

"Eight?" The whites of his eyes widened around whiskey colored circles.

Iris chuckled softly. "It was an easy bake oven and yes, eight."

"Wow." Eric shook his head. "What was my sister thinking leaving the kids to me? I don't know anything at all about raising the rug rats."

"You did pretty good today." She had two choices now, sit in the lone easy chair to one side, or slip onto the sofa near him. Intending to shift left to the chair, she found herself instead on the end of the couch, tucking her legs underneath her. "I mean, aside from scaring the hell out of me, you handled the situation well."

"I don't know about that. He's hoarding."

She nodded. "Yeah, I realized that. But it's probably not very unusual. Everything is all new and different for him. He's so little."

"Tell me about it." Eric's head fell back against the sofa. Eyes closed, muscles taut down his neck, she had an odd urge to run her finger along that strong jaw line. His eyes popped open and he turned to face her. "How do parents do this day in and day out? Your grandmother told me not to worry, that no child comes with a handbook, but what if they wind up in therapy the rest of their lives because of me?"

"They won't."

His brows shot up high on his forehead before he sat up. "You sound awfully sure."

"I am." She grabbed a nearby pillow and hugged it against her. It was all she could think of to resist the urge to reach out and wipe away the creases angling between his brows.

Shifting to raise one knee onto the sofa, he draped an arm across the back. "Care to enlighten me?"

She probably would if the warmth of his knee almost touching hers wasn't scrambling her brain cells.

"Change your mind?" One side of his mouth tilted north in a shaky smile.

"Not at all." Pushing to stand, she walked to the kitchen island and grabbed a cookie out of a glass jar. "You have good instincts—"

"I'm not so sure about that." He came beside her, reaching for a cookie as well, then sank onto the nearby stool.

"And," she continued, doing her best to ignore that he was once again only inches away from her, "you care."

The cookie froze halfway to his mouth. "Of course I care. They're Adele's kids."

"It's more than that. You want them to be normal. You want them to be happy. You disobeyed the therapist's instructions, followed your gut, and bought them books. Why? Because you have instincts that told you books are good. Maybe because you enjoyed them with your parents as a kid, maybe because you read an article a thousand years ago and don't remember. Doesn't matter why, what matters is you cared enough to do what was right."

He stared at the cookie as if it held the final word.

"Why did you take them fishing?" she asked.

Eric tore his gaze away from the cookie and focused on her.

"Want me to tell you?" She smiled.

"Because it made me feel good as a kid," he supplied, putting the cookie down.

"And…"

"And I thought it might give us common ground."

She nodded and grabbed his cookie. "See? You care."

"That was mine!"

Hefting one shoulder in a lazy shrug, she bit into the cookie, mumbling, "You snooze, you lose."

He pointed to the now empty glass jar. "And the last cookie."

"Oops." Breaking the cookie in half, she said, "I'm willing to share."

"Oh, gee. Thanks."

"Seriously, though." She handed him the broken cookie. "I think you love those kids more than you realize. Probably have for years even though you don't see them often."

Extending his hand, he accepted the proffered treat and she almost jumped back when his fingertips brushed against hers. When was the last time she'd had this response to a man? Wasn't that thought laughable? She wasn't at all sure any man had ever had this effect on her. The real question was what the heck was she going to do about it.

• • • •

There was no denying Iris was a beautiful woman. Heck, from what he'd seen so far there wasn't an ugly Hart granddaughter in the bunch, but keeping his thoughts to himself was becoming increasingly difficult.

He hadn't meant to touch her. Not that most people would consider a brushing of fingertips for a brief second or two touching, but he'd felt the jolt all the way to his toes. And from the startled look in her eyes, so had she. Which left one remaining question, what was he supposed to do about it?

"I, uh," Iris shifted away, her gaze landing on the crackling logs, "need to check the fire."

All he could do was nod. Then he cursed himself for noticing well rounded hips when she squatted in front of the burning wood. What would have happened had they met under different circumstances? No kids? No sadness? Just two people, at a romantic lake, under the spring skies.

"How is Richard's family taking all this?" She poked at the smoking fire.

"I don't know. I haven't talked to any of them."

"Not even at the funeral?" She pushed to her feet and brushed her hands quickly.

"There wasn't a funeral."

The crinkle in her forehead spoke more than any words.

"At least I don't think there was."

"You don't think?" Confusion twisted to utter surprise, possibly disbelief.

This wasn't going well. Walking to where she stood, he stopped a foot in front of her. "I was working a rig in the North Sea. I'd just returned home when I got word of the accident. Because it had only been a day or two, the bodies hadn't been released yet, but the kids were packed and ready to board a plane as soon as I answered the phone."

"Who was caring for them?"

"The hotel staff."

"Staff? Wasn't there any friend or family available?"

"I don't know. I assume they had friends but probably not on vacation with them. As for his family, they're very continental. Businesses around the globe. Lots of travel. For all I know they were harder to reach than as I was."

"How many siblings does he have?"

"I hate to keep saying I don't know—"

"But you don't know." She rolled her eyes at him.

He tapped the tip of his nose with his finger. "I know he has at least one or two sisters. Maybe a brother. Or it could have been a brother-in-law. The wedding was a bit of a blur to begin with and frankly, less than thrilled with her new spouse, I may have had a bit much to drink."

"Yeah, that'll do it."

"According to the solicitor, both Richard and Adele gave explicit instructions for the children to be cared for by me. The estate is mired in international legalities, but I'm guessing Adele knew that I wouldn't need interim money to take care of them."

"Not so middle class after all," she teased.

He had to laugh at that one. She was right. He might be a middle class boy at heart, but his bank account was most definitely not. "I suppose eventually I expect to speak with Richard's family, it just hasn't been a priority. Maybe if the children had asked about them I'd have made more of an effort, but I just wanted to get my feet under me first."

"Can't blame you for that." She blew out a heavy sigh, and he could see the hurt in her eyes.

Another reason he found her so blasted attractive. A blind man could see she had a heart for those around her. Whether the love and respect for an aging grandparent or teasing cousin or family friend. She cared. But the heavy sigh? He didn't know if that was for his sister, the kids, him, or something else totally unrelated to him.

"What about your dad and grandfather?" Carefully stepping around him, she set the poker back in place. "How are they taking things?"

"Good question. I've spoken with both. I think we're all in shock still. More worried about the kids than ourselves. I considered going to Florida but once the postcard showed up we all agreed that if Adele and Richard had booked a trip here it might be better for the kids than to be surrounded by grieving men they barely know."

"So they don't have any closer relationship with your side of the family than with Richard's?"

He shook his head. "I think that was starting to change, but no."

"I don't understand that." She dropped into the sofa and grabbed the cushion again. "I couldn't fathom not having my grandparents, or my aunts, or cousins. I mean, maybe not so many." She laughed. "But having them and not really knowing them?"

He collapsed into the sofa beside her. "We don't get to choose who we're related to. The way Emily has taken to you and your grandmother, I'm betting she'd rather be related to you guys than me."

"Don't sell yourself short." Her hand landed on his arm and much to his surprise, unlike the cookie incident, she didn't pull away.

"So," he drew in a slow deep breath, "if I'm supposed to be able to handle all this, what do you suggest I do about the hoarding?"

Iris swallowed hard. "Probably the same thing you have been. Show him love. Show him stability. Sympathy. And things should change. He won't feel so out of control."

"Out of control." Right now he felt like he was in a whirlpool getting sucked underwater. Because like it or not, his self restraint was pretty much gone. Leaning closer, he did his best to read in her eyes if his next move would be welcome or send him packing. He hoped he'd gotten it right. Another inch and his lips met hers. Soft, sweet, and then she leaned forward and his heart did a somersault. He wasn't sure who moved first. Whose arm wrapped around who. But he could feel her heart beat against his and didn't want to ever let go.

The fire crackled. A log snapped. And reluctantly, he loosened his hold on her waist as she pulled away. Thankful her hands remained resting on his shoulders.

"Should I apologize?" he asked softly.

A glimmer of a smile teased at one side of her mouth. "For what?"

He shook his head and taking one hand into his, rubbed the back of hers with his thumb. "The best damn kiss I've ever had."

"For the record."

He nodded.

"Ditto."

"Then," he glanced at their joined hands then up to her eyes, "it's safe to say, we can do it again?"

The sound of giggling children carried from outside the door.

Straightening her spine, Iris inched back to her side of the sofa. "I sure hope so."

Waiting for the front door to burst open and children and friends to cascade in, one thing came to mind: he should have jumped in the lake much sooner.

CHAPTER FOURTEEN

"You can do it!" Gavin cheered.

"Go Uncle Eric!" Emily shouted over her little brother.

It had taken two days after the boat incident before Lucy stopped fussing enough for Eric to go jogging on the trails. After a visit from Cole one day, Eric was invited to join him at the gym to work out with some of his firefighting buddies. No surprise to anyone the guys got along like fire and oxygen. Next thing Iris knew, training had shifted from jogging to bicycles. Since Cole and his partner had a couple of days off between shifts, the three men had progressed to doing the five mile bike rides together.

Then things got serious. After a friendly round of cards one night, casual male bonding had shifted into multiple boasts of who was in better shape and who had the tougher job. Firemen or deep sea divers.

What should have been another simple marathon on bikes this morning had morphed into a full on triathlon with the cheering squad tagging along behind in the General's Jeep.

From ahead, Eric raised his arm with a thumbs up. The three men were jogging along at a steady pace, none making any effort to pull out in front. Though Iris suspected they were merely pacing themselves. Once they hit the lake for the swim, someone was bound to come out ahead.

"Why isn't Uncle Eric running any faster?" Gavin asked from the back seat.

Emily rolled her eyes at her brother, shook her head, and blew out an exaggerated huff. The kid either had been watching too much TV or had a natural dramatic flair. "Because he doesn't want to make them look bad. Uncle Eric is a nice guy."

A nice guy was hitting the nail on the head, Iris thought. Smart too. And easy on the eyes. Well, they were all easy on the eyes, but she was partial to the one with the whiskey brown eyes, wavy chestnut hair, and killer smile.

From the passenger seat, Lily put her pinkies in the corners of her mouth and let go an ear piercing whistle. Without looking back, Cole gave a fist pump. The man knew his whistles.

"They're nuts, you know that, right?" Lily leaned back in her seat, grinning from ear to ear.

"But you love him anyway." Iris smiled at her cousin. The woman practically glowed.

"Show 'em how it's done, Payton!" Cindy leaned forward between her sister and cousin. "Can't let the poor guy feel left out."

"It was nice of you to tag along to cheer him on," Lily said over her shoulder.

"It only seemed fair. Eric has the two kids and Iris by default."

"Default?"

"Whatever you want to call it. And Payton didn't have anyone. I figure this is the least I can do to support our local firefighters."

"Doesn't hurt that this particular local firefighter is built like a brick house." Lily giggled like a school girl.

Cindy rolled her eyes. "Don't go all romantic on me. As nice as all of Cole's buddies are, I prefer brain over brawn."

"Hey!" Lily twisted in her seat. "Cole has plenty of brain."

"So does Payton," Cindy agreed, "but you have to admit there's a lot of brawn in that testosterone filled mega-chest."

No one could argue that with Cindy. Payton could easily portray the Hulk if he wanted. Not an ounce of fat on the guy, he was all muscle.

"How much further do they have?" Lily asked.

Iris glanced at her odometer. "One more mile."

"So far so good," Cindy added.

Her cousin Cindy was one of the many reasons Iris couldn't imagine not having family. The woman had a heart of gold when it came to animals, was always there for family and even though she didn't technically have a horse in this race, she'd given up her day off to support a friend. Iris was damn lucky when it came to her family.

Cheers sounded from the shoreline below. The guys were winding around Hart House and down hill to the crowd waiting with water, wet suits and plenty of encouragement.

"Good grief." Iris glanced at her wrist watch. "What is everyone doing here at this hour?"

A table had been set up with drinks and fruit and Lucy was at the helm with Aunt Virginia, ready to rehydrate the troops. Ralph and Floyd were with the General yacking away, waving American flags. Car doors slammed behind them and Iris spotted Callie hurrying down the hill with a couple of girls from the volleyball team.

"I'm surprised the whole town isn't showing up." Cindy waved at her sister and hopped out of the car as soon as Iris shifted into park. "Who are you rooting for?"

"All of them," Callie answered, hurrying down the hill.

Emily and Gavin ran to catch up to Lily in the front. "Miss Lucy said we could help hand out the fruit."

"Yeah," Gavin smiled up at her. "We helped her cut it up last night."

"Only a little," Emily corrected. "Miss Lucy and Grams cut the big pieces first and we got to use the plastic knives to cut them up smaller."

"That was very nice of you," Poppy said coming up on the rear.

Iris loved that the kids had relaxed so much in the days since the fight over Cheetah on the water that they'd actually begun calling her grandmother Grams. After all, why not? Everyone else did. They'd also begun to use Uncle Eric more regularly verses merely speaking without a name. And this morning, for the first time since Cheetah was washed and dried and fluffed, Gavin willingly left him in the cabin. What a difference in such a short while.

"Can we run ahead?" Emily asked.

Iris nodded. "Go on, but not too fast."

"Right." Cindy laughed. "Like that ever worked with any of us."

"Hey, I have to try. It's an adult's job."

"I don't know," Lily shrugged, "four adults here and you were the only one to pull the mom card."

Mom card? Was that what she'd done. No. She'd been a nanny for years, it was the nanny card. Old habits hard to break, and that sort of thing. But her cousin was right about one thing, she wasn't on the job here, and she wasn't their mom. She wasn't really anything, except unemployed.

The kids reached the table at nearly the same time as the three men. A bunch of high fives abounded, but Eric was the only one to lose time by hugging each of the kids before shimmying into the wet suit and running after the other two men into the water. Her heart did a little jig. Who was she kidding. She wasn't merely adulting, she loved those kids. And good or bad, she loved the man that came with them. Oh, boy.

● ● ● ●

Water was easy for Eric. Swimming to the buoy and back put him ahead of the others without any effort. Pacing himself always won the battle. Whether he was up against a rig in the North Sea, Australia, or a couple of firemen on a mission. What he wasn't used to was a welcoming committee on the shore.

He was pretty sure he hadn't noticed this many people when he'd rushed into the lake. Had Nadine and Katie been here? Lucy and the kids were once again at their post with bottles of spring water in hand. Just the sight of the half pints gave him an energy boost.

"Here you go!" Emily held out the bottle, a grin taking over her face. "The General says you have to hurry."

"Here they come!" Gavin pointed to the water behind him.

Eric ruffled Gavin's curly hair. "Thanks, sport." Jogging up hill, he waved to Nadine and Katie as the two women whistled and cheered.

At the ready by the bikes, Iris stood with her cousins. Unzipping his suit as he approached, he climbed out of it, handed it off to Iris's waiting hand, and reached for the handlebars.

"We'll follow behind you." She smiled.

He resisted the urge to pull her in for a quick kiss and nodded. "Thanks."

Tipping her chin toward the lake, she waved him on. "You'd better hurry. Here they come."

"That's what Gavin said." He smiled and climbing onto the bike, foot on the pedal, took off up the rest of the hill. Minutes later, the three men were cycling across Hart land, the Jeep with Iris, the kids and her two cousins following behind.

How things had changed in such a short time. When he'd first brought the children to his home he couldn't fathom anything ever being normal again. Actually, Eric couldn't fathom life with two children as normal either. Already, he couldn't fathom life without them. In only a few weeks everything about his new family seemed perfectly normal, and so did everything about the lake. Well, the cabin was a tad on the tight side, but still, growing up should be all about playing Jacks, and finger painting, and rock hunting, and fishing, and swimming in the creek, and a million other things that big city kids missed out on.

Adults missed out on a lot too. Like late night card games, and checkers at the barber shop, and workouts with new friends, or impromptu triathlons with firemen. Speaking of which, Payton's front tire edged up closer to him.

"Not on your life, buddy," he muttered to the wind, leaning forward, and pushing a little harder. The time had come to hold the lead. Over his shoulder he could hear the kids cheering him on. Lily had a whistle that could probably be heard halfway across the county and Cindy must have been a cheerleader in school, but the sweet sound of Gavin reassuring him that he could do this beat the others out hands down. He could do this. In the grand scheme of things, a little friendly competition wasn't that big a deal but in the eyes of his nephew and niece, he was the better man and he had no intention of disappointing them.

Winding around the last section of road, he cycled back to Hart House. This time Eric was positive there were more people milling about. From the main entrance folks were lined up, waving flags and cheering as though he and the others had returned from war and not a short two wheeled ride.

He could almost feel the breath of the rider behind him. Sneaking a peek over his shoulder, he could see Payton and Cole neck and neck, and less than a bike length or two behind. Ahead, the General and Mrs. Hart held the ribbon across the main road onto Hart Land. He could do this. Pumping faster than he had all day, he turned onto the property, whirled past the trail of cheering people and ripped through the massive red ribbon. Gavin's gleeful cheers could be heard loud and clear.

"Job well done." The General came up beside him and slapped him on the back.

Ralph came rushing over. "I'll take charge of the bike."

"Here you go." A few short steps behind Ralph, Lucy came running up holding a water bottle for him, and two more for Cole and Payton.

"Rematch," Cole and Payton echoed.

"Any time." Eric laughed. "More than happy to teach you boys a lesson."

"Oh, them's fighting words," Cole teased.

"Now now boys. Put the measuring sticks away." Grams shook her head, and Eric almost spit his water out. Had those words actually come out of Mrs. Hart's mouth? The woman was the picture of eccentric charm; he'd have expected a comment like that from Lucy or the General, not from the General's wife.

Doors slammed and the entourage that had followed them on the road poured out onto the beach.

"You won." Gavin bounced in place. "Does this mean we get extra ice cream now?"

Eric almost roared with laughter. The kid had a one track mind when it came to ice cream. "You'll have to ask Miss Lucy, but I'm guessing the answer will be yes."

"Ask me what?" Lucy returned from the folding table with more bottled water in hand.

"For extra ice cream tonight," Eric explained.

"Of course." Lucy nodded, and before anyone could say much more, she waved a thumb over her shoulder. "You have company also."

Lifting his gaze toward the house, a tall lean woman in crisp pleated slacks and a long sleeve button down shirt, who looked like she'd fallen off the cover of a major fashion magazine, came his way.

Eric squinted against the sun. He was pretty sure the woman was stunning. He also felt confident that she was staring straight at him, and not at anyone else in the area.

"Roberta Hughes." She extended her hand. "We finally get to meet again."

Again? Eric knew he was gaping. Except for the long lashes and carefully applied makeup, he was staring at a female version of Richard. Bloody hell. What did she want?

CHAPTER FIFTEEN

I ris resisted the urge to tell Eric to close his mouth or he'd catch flies. It took a few seconds for him to snap his jaw on his own and mumble, "Hello."

"You are not an easy man to reach." She turned to Iris and her cousins, extending a hand to each. "How do you do? I'm Gavin and Emily's aunt."

"How do you do," Iris answered first. "Iris Colby."

In turn, each of her cousins introduced themselves as more people came up ignoring the overdressed female, slapping Eric on the back, shaking his hand, followed by Cole and Payton.

Payton practically knocked Eric off his feet when his beefy hand landed on Eric's shoulder. "Good job! If you ever want a second career, we can always use a good man at the station."

"Station?" Roberta's gaze not-so-subtle traveled from head to toe and back. A twinkle appeared in her eye.

Iris may not know if she liked the woman yet, but at least she knew the lady had good taste.

"Yes, ma'am." Payton beamed. "Firefighter Payton Taylor at your service."

"Oh, my," Roberta mumbled softly, before turning to Cole. "And you are?"

Lily sidled up beside Cole, hooked her arm through his and smiled broadly. "Taken."

"Nice to meet you." Cole extended his free hand before waving at Lily. "Have you met my fiancée?"

Roberta nodded and for the first time since the scramble of people began gathering, noticed Emily and Gavin at either side of their uncle hanging tightly to his legs. "I see you have gained new appendages."

To her credit, the woman sank to the ground, resting her weight on her pristine and pricey leather shoes. Red soles and all. Iris still couldn't decide if she liked her or not. The shoes were a waste, the squatting was a plus. The smile was still to be determined.

"You probably don't remember me," Roberta said softly.

Both children tightened their grips on their uncle as his hands fell protectively on their shoulders.

"I'm your dad's sister."

Neither child responded.

Roberta seemed to wobble slightly, her smile faltering. "Well." She appeared to consider saying something else before sighing and pushing to her feet.

"I guess it's been a while," Eric said.

"Mm," she nodded, glancing around at the mad rush of activity.

All around them, folks were still laughing and shouting and scurrying about as Lucy and others brought out tables and chairs and set up for what Iris knew was going to be a fun-filled afternoon of food and games. Maybe.

"I seem to have come on a big day," she said, easing her sunglasses from the top of her head onto the bridge of her nose. "But I would like to discuss something important with you. Could you spare a minute?"

Eric looked down at the two children and then up. "Now isn't really a good time."

"It really is important," she repeated.

"Did you show your uncle what we made for him?" Grams came floating up to them.

Emily shook her head, but Gavin kept his eyes on his newly discovered aunt.

"In that case, come along. We'll bring it to him. And I believe someone mentioned something about extra ice cream too." Smiling, Grams held out her hand.

"Go on with Grams." Eric nudged the children forward. "I'll join you for the winners' ice cream in a few minutes."

Slowly, Emily eased her hold on her uncle and accepted Grams' proffered hand. Gavin followed his sister and the three walked away, Grams leaning forward sharing secrets as they walked. For just a minute Iris remembered being a little girl, walking with her Grams to pick berries, her grandmother sharing some innocuous little secret and

Iris feeling like the favorite granddaughter. Grams had a way of making each of them feel they were special. Iris had no doubt she was doing that now with Emily and Gavin.

"Grams?" Roberta enunciated slowly.

"She's my grandmother," Iris answered. "The children are very fond of her."

"I see." Roberta watched the trio disappear into the house then spun around. "Is there some place private we can go?"

"We should see if Lucy needs any help." Lily steered Cole toward the folding tables on the Point.

"Good idea." Cindy smiled and hooked her arm through Payton's. "Come on, big boy."

"Flattery will get you everywhere," the playful fireman replied.

As much as she wanted to stick around, Iris eased back a step. "I'll see if Grams needs any help."

"No." Eric snatched her arm. "Stay."

Feeling the heat and strength of his grip, she glanced quickly from his hand up to his eyes, the intensity of his gaze held her in place.

"Please," he whispered.

Iris gave a single affirming dip of her chin. She didn't know what was going to happen, but right now, she would have agreed to march into hell and back with this man.

• • • •

"Can we at least sit somewhere?" the woman asked.

"Of course. Sorry." Eric looked around and taking hold of Iris's hand, strolled across the way to a picnic table under a thatch of trees. Somewhere in the back of his mind he knew he'd have to deal with Richard's family sooner or later but he'd expected it to be later. At least until he had a better handle on things. Important things like where would he live? Where would the kids go to school? How would he deal with work absences? Never mind trivial things like learning to cook balanced meals, appropriate bedtime stories, and the myriad of details he still didn't know enough about to even know he didn't know.

"The children looked happy." She slid into the seat. "At least until I tried to talk to them."

"They've been through a lot." He eased onto the bench beside Iris, but didn't let go of her hand. When he reached for her, he was delighted when her fingers curled around his. In such a short time, she'd become an important part of his new world. From the minute she'd ordered him to sit on the boat he'd known that whatever came to pass, he wanted Iris to be a part of it.

"They have." Her gaze dropped to her folded hands. "Richard changed after he married Adele." She lifted her eyes to meet his. "Just a little at first. Simple things. So subtle I almost didn't notice. He was just a tad more… thoughtful. But when Emily was born and I saw Richard changing diapers," she smothered a chuckle, "I knew the brother I grew up with was gone."

Had the man really changed? Eric hadn't noticed. Or maybe he didn't give the guy a chance. Last year when they'd gone on a family vacation both Richard and Adele had invited him to join them. He'd been flying from one end of the world to the other and simply couldn't make the dates work. Maybe he should have tried harder.

"Anyhow, we had a chance to chat when they returned home from vacationing here at the lake last year. Richard seemed to have a new appreciation for the American perspective. It came as a bit of a surprise to hear they were considering relocating to this part of the world. Under the circumstances it made sense for them to appoint you as guardian."

"So you knew?" He remembered his sister talking to him about it, but he hadn't really taken it to heart. After all, no one expects to lose their younger sister before her children had time to grow up.

"I knew. So did my sister."

He nodded. It made sense that Richard would tell his family. Things like that weren't usually secrets. "You didn't come all this way to tell me that, did you? Or are you just here to see if I'm totally screwing up?"

"No. Well, not really."

"No or not really?"

"No." Roberta straightened her spine, not that she'd done anything close to slouching. "Your sister had a great deal of faith in you, but it's nice to see for myself that the children are comfortable with you."

"You didn't expect that?"

She shrugged. "Let's just say none of us saw the children as often as we could have."

There was no point in arguing with her, they both knew she was right.

"Have you made any plans?"

"We're still working things out."

"You have a one bedroom apartment. What are you going to do about that?"

"I'm considering my options." And he was. That much was the truth. Still, he didn't know if he liked that she knew that about him.

"And school? Emily is missing classes, isn't she?"

"Gavin is preschool age, he's fine. According to the records the solicitor sent me, Emily is considerably ahead of the average first grader here in the US, she'll have no problem taking time off now and starting second grade on schedule."

Roberta nodded. "I'm not surprised. Not only is she a smart kid, but that's something our father always harped on. Why would any of us want to study in the USA when the British education is so far ahead."

He'd learned all about that in the two hour long conversation with the solicitor. "We have good schools here too."

"I'm sure you do." She reached for the handbag at her side and pulled out a tin box of mints, then held it out to them.

"No thank you," Eric said first, then Iris shook her head.

"You've been hard to get a hold of." She dropped the tin back in her bag. "My brother's solicitor finally gave up your location. The authorities are ready to release Richard and Adele's bodies."

In an odd sort of way, despite having her children here with him, he'd managed to fool himself into thinking of his sister as living her life as usual, merely out of sight, but not really gone. Reality punched him in the chest. Hard. "I see."

"They were unable to reach you."

"Phone service is sketchy here." He should have thought of that. Followed up.

"My parents want them buried in the family crypt." She looked out to the water and back. "Do you have a problem with that?"

"No." They'd chosen England to be their home. That was fine with him.

"That makes things at least a little easier."

For the first time since this woman walked up to him, the hairs on the back of his neck stood on end. "Easier?"

Roberta squeezed her eyes shut a moment and then quickly blurted out, "My parents also want the children to be raised in England. With them."

If his chest hurt a moment ago, it was nothing compared to the pain stabbing his heart at the thought of losing Emily and Gavin. Not even Iris squeezing his hand in support helped ease the shock. One more thing for him to figure out. And fast.

CHAPTER SIXTEEN

"They're still talking." Cindy peered through the blinds. "What do you suppose she wants?"

"I'd rather not speculate." Grams put the lid on the ice cream container. "And lower your voice. I don't want the children to hear you."

Cindy reached for the refills on the children's ice cream. "I'll take those to them."

"Does the General know Richard's sister is here?" Lily asked.

Grams shook her head. "I don't think so."

"Well, maybe one of us should go tell him." Lucy glanced at her phone then pulled a covered plate from the fridge.

"How much more food are you going to put out?" Lily pointed to the plate.

"Oh this?" Lucy did a terrible job of feigning innocence.

"Uh oh." Cindy looked to her cousin. After all these years her matchmaking radar could read Lucy's expressions like the proverbial open book.

"Lucy?" Grams asked.

"It's just a little snack for the guest in the Hickory cabin."

"We have a guest in the Hickory?" Cindy wasn't a part of the day to day business at Hart House, but usually everyone had an idea of all the guests and usually had managed to cross paths at some point. "Recent arrival?"

Grams shook her head. "He's been here for over a week."

"Is he ill?" Lily asked.

Lucy cleared her throat. She didn't look any more convincing that she wasn't up to something. "No, he's fine."

The phone in Lucy's pocket sounded and she turned her back to the room. "Hello… Yes. Everyone is here. Don't forget the pie. That'll be perfect. See you soon."

"Who will we see soon?" Grams asked.

"Thelma." Lucy flashed a satisfied smile and set the dish on the counter.

Hands on her hips, Lily turned to Lucy. "Since when does Thelma bring pie?"

"Oh, well. Uh," Lucy stammered.

Uh oh. None of them had to be a genius to know whatever Lucy was up to had to do with one of the Merry Widows and the guest in the Hickory cabin. She didn't know if she should simply thank her lucky stars that Lucy wasn't trying to match one of them up with some loser, or to run and warn the poor unsuspecting guest that he was about to be Lucy's next target.

• • • •

Iris didn't like the sound of any of this. All she could do was try to reassure Eric with her presence and keep her mouth closed. She really had no place getting involved, but was very glad he'd wanted her to stay.

"Not going to happen," Eric answered without skipping a beat. "Nothing you say or do will convince me to give those children up."

"I'm not trying to."

A couple of teens who'd arrived with Callie came running up to them. "Hot dogs are ready. Burgers will be ready in five." And just like that they tore off toward the house.

"Interesting place," Roberta mumbled, turning back to face Eric. "We read about quaint little towns in sweet novels, or catch a glimpse in a Norman Rockwell picture, but I can't believe places like this really exist."

"Would anyone like something to drink?" Another teen came up with a case in his hands containing chilled cans of soda. "There's beer for the adults if you'd like one."

Roberta took a diet cola and scanned the remainder of the case. "Thank you."

"I'll have one too." Iris smiled at the teen. "And if you have a chance, bring us a couple of glasses."

"Yes, ma'am." The teen bobbed his hand and took off back in the direction he came from, crossing paths with Louise Franklin who waved a stack of cups at him.

Iris pushed to her feet. "I'd better go get the cups. Be right back."

"Good idea," Eric said.

Too bad she hadn't managed to crawl out from the table before Louise hurried up to them. "The youth of today. They think everyone drinks out of a can or bottle."

"Thank you." Roberta accepted the proffered glass.

"I'm Louise Franklin. I don't believe we've met."

"This is Emily and Gavin's aunt," Eric explained.

Louise's smile slipped. "I'm so sorry for your loss."

"Thank you," Roberta said again.

The three remained perfectly silent and to Louise's credit, rather than push through digging for gossip, she retreated a step. "I was just on my way to check if Lucy needs any help in the house."

Iris nodded and waited for the older woman to be out of ear shot. "That was a close call."

"Close call?" Roberta poured her drink into the glass.

"Small towns are quaint and picturesque but everyone is also sure to know everyone's business. And if they don't they want to know."

"Ah, I see." Roberta set the can down. "But I don't believe you do. I'm not here to convince you to give the children to my parents."

"You're not?" Eric said.

"No. I'm here to warn you. Mum and Dad have been advised to obtain an American lawyer to defend their position." She took a quick sip. "They're in New York as we speak."

"Do you have a lawyer?" Iris asked him. One of the perks of the circles her family, as well as the families she worked for, ran with was connections. Off the top of her head two prominent names came to mind for good family lawyers.

Eric shook his head. "I do have a buddy."

"You'll need a good one." Roberta toyed with the can. "They're going to emphasize that as a single man who travels for a living, you're not equipped to offer the best environment for the kids."

"That's bu...nk."

She had to give him credit, she would have said exactly what she was thinking.

Roberta put her hands up palm out. "You don't have to convince me. Anyone related to Adele has to be at least a little capable—"

"More than a little," Iris defended without thinking.

"All I had to see was the way the kids clung to you earlier to know my brother made the right choice. Heaven knows," she smiled, "if Melissa or I got them they'd wind up neurotic power shoppers."

Iris glanced down at the woman's shoes. She'd known a few power shoppers in her day and there was one thing she was very sure of. She would help Eric any way she could to avoid another generation of Hughes power shoppers. Anything.

• • • •

"Let me see if I understand correctly, you flew all this way to warn me your parents are hiring a lawyer to sue for custody of my niece and nephew." Eric wasn't quite sure he believed this woman yet, but he couldn't figure out why she would lie.

"More than that. Melissa and I want to make sure you keep custody."

"And how do you expect to do that?"

"Well, we don't honestly know yet. We've spent the last week reasoning with them, nagging them, and briefly considered tying them up and throwing away the key."

So at least one person in the Hughes family had a sense of humor.

"I would have told you all this over the phone but you—"

"Are hard to reach. Yes."

"So." She slung her legs over the bench and stood. "I'll let you get back to your celebration. Shall we talk tomorrow and come up with a plan?"

Eric pushed to his feet. "Yes. Thank you."

Stiletto heels and all, she glided easily across the grassy yard and up the hill. They probably taught her and her sister to walk with a book on their head.

"What do you think?" Iris asked.

"I don't know. I can't think of any reason she would come and warn me if she were not sincere. How would tipping me off help her parents?"

"I've been wondering the same thing."

"Do you think she's right?" He shifted to face her. "Will my job and marital status work against me?"

Iris shook her head. "I can't imagine that it would. Today single parents adopt children all the time. Fathers are awarded children over the mother all the time. I think to go against the parents' requests, they'd have to prove you're grossly incompetent."

"I don't know what I'm doing."

"That's not true. You've got a few things to learn, but you're not incompetent."

One side of his mouth tipped up in a weak smile. "You may be biased."

"Maybe. But I'm a good judge of character regardless."

"Up for company?" Cole and Lily walked up holding hands.

Eric nodded. What was that saying about a multitude of counselors? On the other hand, there was the too many cooks in the kitchen thing.

"I gather she didn't bring good news?" Lily asked.

"That's still under discussion."

Lily and Cole sported mirrored looks of confusion.

"Have we moved the party?" The General came up, a plate of cooked hot dogs in hand.

"No, sir," Eric responded. He may have been out of the Navy for a heck of a lot of years, but some habits died hard.

It took a moment of long consideration before the General spoke again. "That look on your face doesn't bode well."

"You wouldn't happen to know a good family lawyer?" he asked, trying to project a little more self confidence than he was feeling.

"Family lawyer?" The General's gaze shifted from Eric to Iris and back.

For the next few minutes, ignoring the bluster of activity around them, Eric filled the old military man in on what had just happened over the last few minutes.

"You want to hand them over?" the General asked.

"Absolutely not." If he were honest, a few weeks ago he would have willingly let anyone else even slightly more qualified raise the children. But that was then and this was now. He was not letting his sister down and he was not letting anyone else raise these kids. Right, wrong, good, or bad, he would be doing his best.

The screen door to Hart House slammed and Eric spotted the kids running down the path, Lucy and Grams behind them and Callie and Cindy behind them.

Swinging his legs around, he came to his feet at the side of the table in time for Emily and Gavin to plow into him full speed ahead. "Where's the fire?"

"Oh, please don't say that," Cole teased. The mood at the table lifting instantly.

"Is that lady gone?" Emily asked.

Gavin gave his best scowl. "I don't like her."

"You don't know her," Eric corrected. "It's polite to refrain from judgments until you know a person better."

Gavin's scowl deepened. Maybe Eric needed to work a bit on increasing the kid's vocabulary or learning four year old speak.

"I don't want her to be my aunt." Emily moved around to stand beside Iris. "Can you be my aunt?"

Iris's eyes rounded bigger than the painted rocks the kids had collected. "I, uh," she looked up at him then back at the children, "I would be proud to have you for my niece." Stretching her arm out, she pulled Gavin into her other side and ruffled his curly hair. "And you for a nephew."

And didn't that create an interesting picture. Family picture.

CHAPTER SEVENTEEN

"Well," the General looked across the lawns to the group of people tossing horseshoes, "I vote for now we enjoy the rest of the day and later we deal with this new situation."

Eric nodded and smiled. "I second that idea."

"Me three," Iris chimed in. Not that anyone had asked her.

The General slapped his hands together and leaned down in front of the children. "And I could use your help with this afternoon's celebration."

Emily spun her head around and looked up at her uncle.

"Sure," Eric said. The smile on his face more genuine.

"Great. Let's go." The General held his hands out and with a turn on his heel, the three moved merrily along.

"I'm having a hard time picturing that man ordering young Marines around." Eric kept his gaze on the General's departing back.

"I'm having a hard time processing that this sweet old man and the demanding general are the same person." Cole wound an arm around Lily's waist. "The guys at the station won't believe what a teddy bear he's become."

"Don't let that gentle demeanor fool you." Cindy came to stand beside Payton. "It's reserved for pre-adolescents."

Payton looked from one person to the next. "Am I the only one worried about what celebration surprise the General has in store for us?"

"Try not to dwell on it." Cole smiled at his buddy. "It'll only drive you crazy."

The group laughed loudly, breaking up the tension that had been hanging in the air.

"Come on." Cindy looped her arm in her cousin's elbow. "Someone needs to find out what Lucy and Thelma are plotting."

"I'm not sure I want to know." The same as all her cousins, Iris knew that whenever Lucy acted secretive or peculiar, it was rarely a good sign for some unsuspecting soul. Add Thelma into the mix and things could get hairy. Like a cue in a movie, Thelma came running up to Lucy. Each woman carried a dish of some kind. Heads together, the two friends murmured something, laughed, nodded and then Louise Franklin hurried from her car to join the group. Smiling like loons, the three women sprinted off toward the cabins on the far edge of the lawn. "I'm not sure what to make of that."

"Neither do I," Cindy shrugged, "but if I had to take a guess, it has something to do with the old adage of the way to a man's heart is through his stomach. Lucy is carrying a covered dish and Thelma should have a pie in her hands. Not sure why they need Louise."

"Pie? Thelma?" Iris clearly had spent too much time away from the lake. Then again, people don't change that much. "That woman has trouble with pre-packaged strawberries and a canister of whipped cream."

"Was Louise carrying anything?" Lily asked.

"Didn't notice. If you join us that would even the odds. Three of them and three of us," Cindy urged.

"We might need reinforcements." Iris watched the three laughing ladies disappear behind a thick of tree.

"Do I want to know what you ladies are whispering about?" Eric came to stand beside them.

"You know how Lucy tends to play matchmaker?" Iris asked.

"Badly," Cindy added.

Eric nodded. In his time at the lake he'd heard the cousins explain, and occasionally complain, about Lucy's misguided efforts at pairing people up. Too often against their wills.

"She's up to something and we were just debating if we should figure out what. If we're right, warning the unsuspecting souls would be the honorable thing to do," Cindy explained.

"Or," Lily stepped away from Cole, "we could mind our own business."

Iris shrugged. "They do say ignorance is bliss."

"Shall we flip a coin?" Cindy asked.

Payton looked from one cousin to the other. "I think I may be put to better use over at the grill. If you folks will excuse me?"

"Just save some for the rest of us," Cole shouted over his shoulder.

"No promises," Payton called back.

Eric scanned the area from the Point where the grills were to the road up the hill. "I don't know about Lucy and her friends, but the crowd is growing."

"That would be Thelma and Louise." Iris smiled at him. "And I vote we should go check on her."

"Did you just say Thelma and Louise?" Eric asked.

"They're harmless," Cole added. "At least as far as I know."

"Yeah, but is Lucy?" Iris asked.

Lily bobbed her head. "We need to boogie."

"Agreed." Cindy nodded.

"Yep. Let's go." Iris stepped closer to Eric. "Would you please come along in case we need reinforcements?"

"Cole?" Lily asked and her fiancé nodded, following after her.

"Wait." Eric fell into step behind Iris and Cindy. "Why exactly are we following Lucy and her friends?"

"You know," Cole spoke softly, "there are times in life when it doesn't pay to ask too many questions. Just remind yourself, 'if mama ain't happy, nobody's happy.'"

Iris quickly muffled a laugh at the utter surprise—and confusion—that took over Eric's face. Even so, he fell into step and didn't question the intelligence of their decision. And just like that, all the troubles of the day slipped away, and Iris only had one thing on her mind. Sharing the lake she loved with Eric and the kids. Except, she wasn't going to let herself consider how long that could last.

● ● ● ●

How anyone expected five people to sneak up unnoticed on Lucy and her friends was beyond Eric, but what did this city boy know.

"Shh." Iris lifted her finger to her lips. "I can see Lucy and the ladies, which means if they hear us they'll see us too."

Lowering his voice, Eric turned to Iris. "Remind me exactly what the plan is?"

"We don't have one," Iris answered softly.

Eric exchanged a baffled glance with Cole.

"Oh look." Cindy pointed. "Louise did bring something. As a matter of fact, it looks like a box from the Pastry Stop."

Lily grinned. "That makes me happy. I think."

"Lucy, Louise and Thelma are definitely up to something." Cindy marched forward.

"Hang on a minute." Eric came to a stop. "Louise and Thelma? Lucy actually has two friends named Thelma and Louise and we're stalking them?"

Iris dropped her hands on her waist. "We are not stalking. We are doing a public service."

Cole tilted his head, facing Eric. "Do you think the judge will see it that way?"

This was by far the most ridiculous thing Eric had been a part of in a very long time. He simply did not understand what these women intended to accomplish. Or what they were trying to prevent. But he was fairly sure that whatever it was, it would not be the end of the world, and he had enough of his own problems to figure out.

Lucy and her friends came to a stop at what looked to be one of the last cabins on the resort portion of the property and knocked on the door.

The five of them continued walking along the edge of the grassy area until Cindy, leading the way, held out her hand to slow them. "I'll be darned. There is not one, but two men standing in the doorway."

Iris leaned over Cindy's shoulder. "Oh, we definitely need to save them."

"From what?" Eric asked.

"Whatever scheme Lucy has up her sleeve," Lily explained.

"Maybe they're just being neighborly?" Cole suggested

The three cousins turned and glared at him as though he had just suggested the world was flat.

"All right," Eric said, "if we're going to knock on the door and drag Lucy and her friends away from the two unsuspecting men, do we at least have an excuse for being here?"

"Oh." Iris frowned. "I hadn't thought about that."

"Me neither," Cindy and Lily echoed.

"Any suggestions?" Lily asked.

Iris waved her arms. "We're simply being cordial. We're here to invite them to join the fun on the Point."

"Perfect." Cindy high-fived her cousin. "Let's go."

Falling in step beside Iris, Eric grabbed hold of her hand. When Iris's fingers laced with his, a smile touched his lips. The simplest of gestures, a throwback to teen years when a mere touch kept a guy on cloud nine for days, was enough reason for Eric to follow this woman anywhere she wanted him to go.

Iris leaned into him. "Tonight, we'll sit down with my grandfather and go over the new dilemma of Adele's in-laws. He'll have an old buddy somewhere who will steer us through this."

"Thanks." He most likely knew someone who knew someone, but he liked the sound of us. Not to mention, quite frankly, he'd spent enough time in the Navy to appreciate the idea of having an entire family at his back. And Eric was quite sure, if nothing else, the General and his clan would have his back.

Cindy rapped on the door and took a step back.

The purple cabin door drew open, and Lucy stood in the doorway looking about as surprised as Eric must have just a short while ago. "What are all of you doing here?"

"We thought we'd invite the guests to join the fun on the Point." Iris waved her thumb over her shoulder. "Help celebrate the guys' triathlon success."

"Who is it Lu…cy?"

Eric had to blink at the sight of the older, balding man in jeans and a t-shirt emblazoned with *Never underestimate an old man who defended your country*. "Gramps?" he managed to eek out.

His grandfather sighed. "Nice to see you."

Lucy's head snapped left to right and back, taking in the two men. Clearly she was as surprised by the recent revelation as Eric had been. "Then that means…"

Another man stepped into the light and Eric figured he had to be dreaming.

"That would make me Eric's dad. Yep. I see you're holding up pretty good, son."

Eric looked from his father to his grandfather standing on either side of Lucy. "What the hell are you two doing here?"

"You didn't think we were going to leave you alone, did you?" His grandfather turned to Iris. "And thank you for being so helpful with my grandson and great grand children. This hasn't been an easy time for any of us."

Iris bobbed her head. "I'm sorry for your loss, but it has been my pleasure. Emily and Gavin are lovely children."

"I don't understand." None of this was computing for Eric. "How long have you been here?"

His grandfather had the decency to look contrite. Eric wasn't sure he wanted to hear what the answer was going to be.

"You didn't honestly think we'd leave you to deal with everything on your own? Your dad and I got here the day after you did. We've been keeping an eye on you. Wanted to be near if you needed us." The man lifted his chin and smiled. "But you didn't."

"Well. I think it's time we get back to the Point. People are probably looking for us. Don't you think, Cindy?" Lily elbowed her sister. "Cindy?"

"Oh." The startled blonde took a step in retreat. "Yes, of course. Payton is probably eating the last of the hot dogs and hamburgers as we speak."

"No sense in hiding out here anymore now that the cat is out of the bag." Eric's father stretched his arm out the doorway and looked to the three women still standing in the cabin. "We might as well all join the party now."

Eric's grandfather, father, Thelma, Louise, and Lucy walked past him and out the door. Cindy, Lily and Cole were several steps ahead when Iris turned to him. "Are you okay?" she asked.

His gaze followed his father and grandfather walking down the hill. None of this made any sense to him. Not his family hiding out to spy on him, and not Richard's sister coming to warn him about her parents. All in all, he wasn't sure who had the crazier family. Squeezing Iris's hand, he shook his head. "I honestly haven't a clue."

CHAPTER EIGHTEEN

Today was proving to be a very odd day indeed. This morning when Iris woke up, the day's plan was clear. Eric and Cole and Payton were going to run and swim and bike the morning away. She and the kids would cheer them on, and her family and friends would be there for him the same way they'd been there since his arrival as he grew more comfortable in his role of uncle to two kids.

Now, not only had the children's paternal aunt come to meet them, the aunt had dragged Richard's parents into the mix. Not a pleasant mix either. And then, before they even had time to process what the anticipated appearance of the British grandparents would mean to Eric and the kids, his dad and granddad showed up. Well didn't actually show up, apparently they've been here all along. And didn't that confuse everything. But it did explain why the guests in the Hickory cabin were keeping a low profile. What she hadn't a clue about was exactly who Lucy was trying to match up with who, because Iris had no doubt that woman had a plan. The last thing Eric needed now was Thelma and Louise for step-parent and grandparent.

"A penny for your thoughts?" Eric asked quietly.

Iris hefted a lazy shoulder. "I'm confused."

"Join the club."

"Is this typical for them?"

He shook his head. "For one thing, they haven't left Florida in ages. If they're not home, they're in the Keys fishing. We see each other every year at either Christmas or Thanksgiving unless I get called away, but not much more than that. This last year we did Thanksgiving the three of us. Adele and Richard spent Christmas with them. I was able to visit for a couple of days at the end of their trip. We rang in the New Year together."

"Was that when your sister told you about making you the children's guardian?"

"Actually, it was last summer. I suspect after visiting this place."

"Really?" Iris wondered if he was correct in his assumption.

Eric slowed his steps, letting the others get a head start. "I think deep down I noticed that there was a difference in the tone of our conversations after their vacation here. Of course at the time I just knew they'd gone to a lake in New England. Richard had mentioned more than once what a lovely time they'd had. I have to admit, the last conversation I had with him, he was obviously less uptight. I suspect this place turned the tide for him about life in the United States verses life in England and his kids' upbringing."

"What are you going to do now?"

"Talk to Dad and Grandpa. First chance I get, we're going to slip away and I'm going to get some answers."

"Left, right, left." The General's voice carried from Hart House to their right. "That's it, troops!"

"Uh oh." Iris rolled her eyes. "That's his footlocker. Is it a full moon or something? Maybe it's written in the stars that grandfathers are supposed to drive their grandchildren nuts today."

"In my case that would be fathers and grandfathers. What's the General doing with his foot locker?"

"That's what I want to know. But like we all can read Lucy, I can tell when that old man is up to something."

"Give me a hand here!" the General called to Eric. "Been saving this for the right time. I think this is it."

Letting go of her hand, Eric trotted over to where the General held the old marine trunk on one end and the kids shared the handle on the other side. "Where are we going with this?"

"Down the hill. I think by the wall will be a good spot for us. Plenty of camouflage."

Camouflage? Iris looked up. Even though it was broad daylight, she wondered if there wasn't a big old white full moon shining down on them. Nothing.

"And here we go. This is nice and close to the water but away from the sand."

Emily and Gavin were practically jumping out of their skins with excitement. If Iris guessed correctly, the two were in on the General's mischief.

"Can I pick first?" Emily asked, grinning from ear to ear at the old man she'd grown fond of.

"Then me?" Gavin added enthusiastically.

The General gave the boy a reassuring pat on the shoulder. "You two will get first pick."

Jumping up with excitement, both kids cheered. At that moment Emily turned to face the General and froze in place. Iris lifted her gaze to follow where the child was looking, and spotted Eric's grandfather smiling at her.

"Grampy!" Emily took off at a fast dart as her great grandfather opened his arms to meet her halfway.

"How's my buttercup?"

Immediately she prattled on all that happened without slowing for a breath. "And then Uncle Eric took us fishing. Except we didn't have time to fish before we dropped Gavin's bag in the water."

"Oh no," the old man said gravely.

"It was okay. Uncle Eric diveded in after it."

"Good for Uncle Eric."

Emily grabbed hold of one hand and Gavin of the other, and together they dragged the old man to where the General stood by the footlocker.

"What have we here?" Their grampy came to a stop.

Turning to face the voices, the General's eyes rounded for a flash in time before he cleared his throat and flipping the locker lid open, announced, "A little afternoon fun."

Eric's grandfather dropped his gaze to the contents and let out a belly laugh. "Now that is my kind of fun."

Iris looked down at the chest filled with every size water gun imaginable. Old fashioned squirt guns, super soakers, fireman soakers, streamers, blasters, and everything in between.

"Come on." Eric's granddad handed Gavin a water gun almost as big as he is. "You can be on the Navy team like your uncle and me. We'll show these Marines how it's done."

"That'll be the day." The General handed a gun to Emily. "We'll show them, won't we?"

Iris watched the interaction. From the communication, it looked to her like maybe she and Eric were the only ones who hadn't known his grandfather was here.

"Pick your teams," the General called out. "Last man dry wins."

"I'm in." A hot dog in one hand, Eric's dad came hurrying over waiving the other. "I'm with Dad and Eric."

Emily threw her arms around Eric's dad. From the way Eric had described his family dynamics, all this affection from the children for their grandfathers wasn't what Iris had expected. Then again, nothing today was going the way she'd expected. A sinking feeling deep in the pit of her stomach told her that the world had just shifted on its axis. After today, everything would probably be very different. The recent happy days of fun and games with Eric and the children looked to be coming to an end.

● ● ● ●

Every time Eric suspected the day couldn't get any stranger, fate stepped in to surprise him. Who knew the General kept a stash of water guns for liquid battle. Only a retired Marine Corps General would keep enough weaponry on hand to start an aquatic war. As each of the participants loaded up their water guns, others on the Point noticing the activity eagerly came to join the fun.

So far they had three teams. Navy, Marines, and first responders. All sprinkled with friends and family. In some ways it reminded him of gym class in school where everybody had to pick who was on their team, but unlike his youth, no one was left out. Torn between her love for her Grampy and Grandpops, and the man who had come to mean as much to her these last couple of weeks, Emily finally opted to battle at Iris and the General's side, with her biological grandfathers assuring her there would be no favoritism. The phrase all is fair in love and war got tossed around a time or two, but Eric had a feeling Emily would be treated like precious cargo anyhow.

Standing in place, considering the new battleground, a sudden spit of icy water hit him in the arm.

"Oops." Standing over Gavin, squirt gun in hand, Thelma flashed an un-apologetic smile. "Just showing the young man how it works."

"Ah!" Thelma squealed and whipped around to catch Louise

holding her weapon to one side.

"Sorry." Her friend shrugged. "Testing the trigger."

Eric bit down on his back teeth and swallowed a laugh. He was starting to think maybe Thelma and Louise were more deserving of their names than he'd given them credit for. Those two definitely deserved each other.

A foil covered tray in hand, Lucy came walking down the path. Mrs. Hart, dressed in a bright ankle length dress and carrying a similar sized tray, followed behind her.

"Joining us, dear?" the General asked his wife. As if confirming the request, two happy and wet golden retrievers barked at Fiona Hart.

"Maybe next time." His wife smiled at him.

Grinning, the General nodded and raised his gun. "The boundaries for the battle ground are from the Sycamore cabin to the Willow, to the Elm, over to the Birch. Refill zones are anywhere along the shoreline and the creek as well as the rain barrels scattered around some of the cabins. Your objective: Soak all opponents. The rules…" He paused to survey the teams crowded around him, and his already contented smile brightened even more to match the twinkle in his eyes. "There are none."

Lucy came marching across the lawn toward the main house. "There's one rule." She waved a finger at the General. "Anyone who shoots at me or Mrs. Hart while tending to the rest of this crowd won't be sitting at our kitchen table for a month."

Multiple heads nodded and a few people winced. Lucy had just ensured that everyone playing kept their guns pointed at anyone but her or the General's wife.

"So," the General slung his super soaker gun over his shoulder and slapped his hands together, "are we ready?"

Questions on soaking, headshots, and eliminations came flying at the General. His attention snagged away by the sound of two doors slamming, it took Eric a moment to recognize the tall blonde descending the hill in jeans as Richard's sister. Earlier she could have fallen off the cover of any high fashion magazine. Now, she could have easily been on the cover of Fish and Stream. He could only assume the other lady rushing to keep up with Roberta's quick pace was her sister. Now what?

Having spotted the women at the same time, even though she and he were on separate teams, Iris came hurrying over to stand beside him, her gaze quickly scanning Roberta's more appropriate attire.

"Don't look so surprised," Roberta said in a rush, "even we Brits know how to dress for a picnic."

"Sorry, I didn't mean—"

Roberta held her hand up. "No offense taken. But there's been an update. We need to talk."

"Okay." A spare gun in each hand, the General called out in full Marine Corps command mode. Eric hadn't noticed the General approaching, and his jaw almost hit the floor when the family patriarch handed one to each sister. "We're starting. Pick a side and get moving. Y'all can talk later." He spun around. "And go!"

To his surprise, Roberta looked left then right at the brigade of people scrambling for cover while firing spouts of water, and grabbing her sister by the hand, crouched and headed for a wall of shrubs shouting, "You Yanks do throw an interesting party."

He was just thinking the same thing.

CHAPTER NINETEEN

Apparently the General's free for all rules meant even those soaked to the bone were still allowed to play. Iris and her cousins had one advantage over many of the guests: they knew all the best spots for ambushing unsuspecting opponents. While she'd been hit a few times, compared to some of the other folks on the team, they were pretty high and dry.

"Okay," Lily crouched behind the hydrangea shrubs, "Eric's grandfather is as bad as the General when it comes to this war zone stuff."

Large hair comb in her mouth, Cindy wrung out her ponytail then clipped it to the top of her head. "Tell me about it. That old guy is like a stealth bomber."

"More like a torpedo," Iris suggested.

"What did he do in the Navy anyhow?" Poppy asked, pressed against the wall.

"All I know is he retired as a captain."

"Captain? That's impressive," Cindy said.

Poppy squinted, eyes to the sky. "What's that in the Marine Corps?"

"Full bird Colonel," Iris answered.

"Oh, that is impressive." Poppy nodded.

"So, what's the plan?" Cindy leaned in.

"Spread the word." Iris huddled with her cousins. "The Navy team is using the back of the Elm as home base. We'll surround them on three sides. When you see me step out in the open, that's the sign they're moving. Everyone count to three and we'll show those squids what a Marine soaking is all about."

"Sounds good," several voices echoed.

Iris made her move around the side of the cabin. The only one of her team dressed in brown, she was able to easily blend in with the foliage and skirt the perimeter. Almost to her objective, Lucy came hurrying down the hill, weaving her way from bush to shrub.

"I think we have a problem." Lucy reached Iris, huffing heavily, her hand to her heart.

Iris seriously didn't like the looks of that. "Are you all right?"

"Fine. I just wanted to reach you before your grandmother and guests track you down."

"Track me down? What are you talking about?"

"Well, if I didn't know any better, I'd say the Queen of England has descended on us."

"Queen of England? Lucy, what in heaven's name are you talking about?"

"The two people insisting on speaking with Eric."

Eric? Uh oh.

"The woman is not only wearing a linen suit, she's wearing stockings. Who wears stockings on a warm day like this? Oh yeah, and sensible black pumps." Lucy shook her head. "Do you know anyone besides the Queen who wears yellow with black shoes?"

"Probably lots of people. Who exactly—"

"Did I mention she has a proper British accent? I don't know about the man with her, she hasn't let him get a word in edgewise."

Sometimes she really needed to learn to skip a few chapters and get to the point. "Lucy. Is it Emily's grandparents?"

The housekeeper's hands landed heavily on her hips. "What do you think I've been telling you. We have to do something."

At the sound of the slamming screen door, pointing her water weapon toward the ground, Iris looked up the hill to Hart House. Lucy had a point. At a distance the female visitor did indeed look like the Queen of England from a decade or two ago. And the dour expression on the woman's face did nothing to ease the knots forming in Iris's stomach.

Walking briskly, her grandmother escorted the Queen and a stately gentleman down the path directly toward the battle zone. *Blast.* Eric would be with the rest of his team and Iris needed to boogie if she wanted to both head off the visitors *and* warn him. Turning to Lucy, she rested her hand on the woman's arm. "Thanks. I'll handle it from here."

"You do that," Lucy said. "I'm going to find the General and his school buddy."

"School buddy?" Iris paused mid-step, momentarily forgetting the urgency of her mission.

"That Navy captain is an Annapolis graduate like your grandfather." Lucy waved over her shoulder and continued hurrying down hill.

Annapolis? Did her and Eric's grandfathers know each other? That was a long shot. Lots of people graduated from Annapolis. But Lucy said buddy. Iris sighed. There was no time to think about it now. She needed to find Eric. But her grandmother was almost upon them. Thinking fast, she decided running interference would give Lucy and her grandfather time to find Eric. Taking off at a quick clip, Iris shot across the open field to catch up with her grandmother when a sudden kaleidoscope of colors flashed from all directions along the perimeter.

The world suddenly turned in slow motion. The Marine team spun around in the open from behind bushes and trees. The Navy team rushed forward, guns taking aim. Iris couldn't have stopped the impending fiasco if the future of the universe had depended on it. Sprays and streams of water shot across time and space as the team members ran back and forth sending massive cascades of water descending around them. Dead center of all the laughter and screeches drowning out the normal pitch of ordinary conversation, the once pristine pseudo Queen of England stood dead center, soaking wet. *Oh, hell.*

• • • •

Oh hell. Eric had seen his sister's wedding photos enough times to recognize the woman with short, curly, salt and pepper hair as Adele's mother-in-law. Her *soaking wet* mother-in-law. For a few very long seconds, Eric stood horrified as gushes of water soared through the air, targeting the oncoming group. Walking in front of Fiona Hart, Anne Hughes had taken the brunt of liquid barrage. Mrs. Hart had suffered only mild collateral sprinkles and Mr. Hughes, still standing behind the two women, remained unscathed from the skirmish.

Only the drenched woman's appalled gasp snapped Eric into action. Bolting full speed ahead, he reached her at the same moment as Iris and the General. Arms extended and eyes circled large and round, Anne Hughes silently surveyed herself. If Eric correctly read the fury in the woman's eyes, any minute she was going to rip him a new one.

"I'll get a towel." Cindy was the first to speak before dashing up the hill.

Fiona Hart came up beside the still stunned woman and sweetly called over her shoulder to her granddaughter. "You'd better make that several towels, dear."

Laughing and smiling, Emily and Gavin came galloping up beside Eric and took position at either side of him, each looping an arm around his middle. From the sudden slip of all merriment from their faces, they too had taken note that their paternal grandmother was most definitely not a happy camper.

"I. Have. Never," the woman managed to huff, looking up at Eric. "I suppose this is all your doing. You've turned my grandchildren into barbarians."

His niece and nephew sidled up even closer to him.

Fiona flashed a disarming smile. "Perhaps we should get you back to the house to dry off."

For the first time in his life, Eric understood the old expression if looks could kill. Clearly, Fiona's attempts to disarm the situation had fallen flat. He also understood why Richard most likely had been such a stuffed shirt. Working all over the world, Eric had met plenty of Brits. Although overall, they generally had a slightly higher standard of polite—what he had often heard mentioned as *British sensibilities*—none quite reached the level of *sensibilities* as Richard and his mother.

Mrs. Hughes turned her steely gaze from Fiona to Eric. "Is this what you consider a proper environment for Emily and Gavin?"

"This," Roberta came to stand beside him, pointing a thumb at her mother, "is what we needed to talk to you about."

Mrs. Hughes quickly scanned her two daughters from head to toe. "And what do you think you are doing?"

"It's called having fun, Mother. You should try it some time."

From a few steps behind, her husband's failed attempt to smother a laugh could be heard, and once again Anne Hughes cast a scathing glare, this time in her husband's direction.

"If you will excuse the pun, I think this is much ado about nothing." The General seemed to be the only person brave enough to plant himself next to the irate woman.

"Agreed." Eric's grandfather came to stand beside the General.

"Mum," Roberta huffed, "until you showed up snapping like a rabid dog, the children were having fun."

Richard's father stepped around his wife and moved forward. "It does appear to me that under the circumstances," reaching Emily and Gavin he stopped and smiled down at them, "the children look very well adjusted."

Emily and Gavin remained still until their grandfather wiggled his fingers hello at them. The effort brought a coy smile to Emily's face, and giggling, Gavin mimicked the wiggling fingers. Unfortunately, Mrs. Hughes didn't appear to agree.

"See," Mr. Hughes said to his wife before his shoulders sank and his smile slipped at his wife's steely gaze.

The General leaned into her. "Perhaps this would be a good time to infiltrate enemy lines."

White lines circled around the dark orbs that matched the gray in Anne Hughes' hair.

"If you'll hear me out," the General continued, "as a military man I can relate to the sense of insubordination that comes with a family who doesn't understand the importance of good order and discipline. Can you imagine how chaotic the royal house would be without protocol?"

The General seemed to be speaking the woman's language. Her deep scowl eased from utter disgust to mere annoyance.

"So many of life's problems come from a lack of unit cohesion. A strong command is key."

The lady actually gave a short nod.

"On the other hand," he raised his fully loaded super soaker, "there are times when the only way to teach the ranks a lesson is to join the battle." He waved his arm that held the water weapon in the general direction of her husband. Without skipping a beat, he handed the water gun to the woman and cocked his head.

The General had to have completely lost his mind. What lunatic would hand the Queen of England a water gun and provoke her to shoot at her husband, the Prince?

"Mrs. Hughes," Eric started, the remainder of his words never fully forming as the edge of the gun lifted upward, the woman retreated half a step and unleashed a full load of water, drenching her husband.

"Actually," Anne Hughes actually cracked what some might call a smile, "you may have something here."

Eric looked to Iris, standing mouth open, staring at the woman now fully grinning at the General, and wondered if maybe he was in reality the only one to have lost his mind.

CHAPTER TWENTY

"I'm not sure I believe today really happened." A glass of lemonade in each hand, Iris sank onto the front stoop and handed one to Eric.

Sitting inches away from her, he accepted the cool drink and shook his head. "I'm not sure I understand what your grandfather did."

Chuckling softly, Iris settled in, resting her elbows on her knees. "He says they communicated."

"Yeah, I heard that too. But I still don't understand."

"Apparently," she explained, "British society matrons and Marine Corps generals have more in common than I realized."

A sweet smiled crossed Eric's lips. "Apparently."

"Well, don't you two look perfectly comfortable." Fiona Hart came up the porch steps. "I've been called to the kitchen. It seems we're expecting a few extra for supper tonight."

Iris started to rise. "I'll help."

"No need." Grams patted her shoulder. "We've got this."

Iris almost swallowed her tongue when Mr. Hughes followed Grams onto the porch—alone—his wife still walking with the General.

"Don't look so alarmed, young lady." Rupert Hughes paused on the steps and smiled at her. "I do believe my Anne has finally met her match."

From where she sat, Iris could see the remnants of activity fluttering down the hill and across the Point. Most of their friends had either called it a day and gone home or joined Lucy and Lily in the kitchen. Only a few remained outdoors enjoying the last remnants of a warm sunny day, the General and Mrs. Hughes being two of them.

After some soft spoken yet heated words, Roberta and her sister may or may not have made peace with their mom. For Iris, a British accent was a bit like a southern accent; no matter the words, everything sounded rather pleasant and polite. Either way, Eric had forced himself to walk away to allow the children time with the other side of their family.

"They seem to be having fun." A trace of melancholy laced his words.

It took Iris a moment to realize he wasn't talking about Anne Hughes and the General but the children and their aunts. Batting away at the tetherball, the children could be heard laughing all the way up the hill.

"They do."

"It's hard to believe how much they've changed in the short time we've been here."

"You're a good uncle," Iris said.

Eric let out a scoffing laugh. "Hardly. Without you and your family I would still be bumbling my way through this and probably setting the kids up for a life of therapy. Hell," he shook his head, "I still might."

"Nonsense. You've had great instincts all along."

"You've said that before. I'm not so sure about that."

"I am." She shrugged. "Besides, love goes a long way and those children love you."

"Maybe, but I sure as hell love them. More than I would have thought." He shifted his gaze from the kids laughing and playing with their aunts to Iris. "If Anne decides to fight me for custody, I'm going to have to make some changes."

"Like?"

"For one thing, I need to find a nine to five, Monday through Friday job."

"Not necessarily."

"At first I thought a nanny like you, or a housekeeper like Lucy would be the perfect answer." He chuckled. "I even hoped to convince you to help me pick someone."

She didn't know if she was honored he wanted her help or offended he didn't want to convince her to take the job.

"Now, I don't think I could leave them for weeks at a time and not worry."

"And yet," she shrugged, "parents do it all the time."

"I don't know that I want to be that kind of parent. Or that Adele would want me to be that cavalier with her children."

"She knew what you do for a living. I'm sure she took all of that into consideration before picking you over Roberta or the other sister or even Richard's mother." Though she imagined any career short of being a serial killer would have beat out Mrs. Hughes for guardianship. Joining the Marine Corps would probably be easier than living under that woman's thumb.

"On the other hand," he said, "I doubt she thought I'd ever actually become guardian. I know I didn't."

The tetherball spun around on the tall pole. Emily stepped in to smack it back around, and Eric pushed to his feet and Iris stood beside him. She'd been right about his instincts, the same sixth sense that had served her well caring for other people's children pricked at her now.

For the second time today, life seemed to pass in slow motion. One of the aunts smacked at the ball, sending it to unwind from the pole. Emily reached up and then swung madly at the ball with both hands. And missed. Unfortunately, the laws of gravity and forward momentum won over balance. The sound of her tiny body smacking against the ground echoed like the crack of a lightening strike.

At Emily's piercing cry, Eric was already halfway down the porch steps. Hitting the ground with a loud thud, he tore off down hill, Iris on his heels.

From inside the house, Grams was already running down the steps and hurrying to catch up to them. She must have seen what happened from a window. Moving quickly, but not breaking into a downright run for what was probably going to be nothing more than a scraped knee and frightened little girl, everyone focused on Emily pushing to her feet. Tears streamed down the little girl's face. Her aunts, only feet away, rushed to her side.

Holding her hands palm up, Emily's tears cascaded in earnest. Completely ignoring the aunts she barely knew, Emily turned, scanning the distance and then taking a slow step forward, cried even louder. With Anne Hughes lurking in the background, this was the last thing Eric needed.

• • • •

A skinned knee. He told himself that was probably all she had. Eric and his sister had gotten worse than that a bazillion times growing up. Then again, he'd also chipped a front tooth taking a fall on the ice hockey rink. Still, his heart hammered in his chest nonetheless.

Crying loud enough for the sobs to carry as clearly as if she were standing next to him, Emily took off running. To his relief, the little girl saw her British grandmother reach out and continued to run past her. Mrs. Hart had veered right along the paved path and was several steps ahead of Eric and directly in Emily's trajectory. Not a surprise that the little girl would run to the sweet older woman. After all, she'd been everything a child could want in a grandmother. Loving, warm, caring, and most of all, fun.

Both Emily and Gavin had developed bonds with all the Hart family members, but just as Gavin loved the General and his dogs, Emily responded to Fiona Hart and her granddaughter Iris.

Fiona's steps slowed as the little girl approached and much to his surprise, he saw Fiona step to one side as Emily zoomed past her. His own pace slowed, taking in the distance between himself and his niece. The General and Anne Hughes were now marching up the hill. Eric's dad and grandfather could be heard coming down the hill behind him. The same as the first day he'd arrived, multiple people were on hand to step in and save the day.

Emily's cries grew louder and Eric felt his heart crack. How did parents do this? How badly would he hurt when she actually broke a bone? Fought with a boy? Lost out on a close call competition? The list of life's painful lessons was longer than his arm and chiseling away at his heart.

Little arms raised up and held out as she took her last steps, closing in on where Iris stood beside him. Wasn't it natural for a little girl to want to be comforted by a woman? So why did knowing Emily would run into Iris's waiting embrace sting so badly?

"It hurts," Emily cried, almost tumbling past Iris and into her uncle.

Folding his arms around her while lifting her up, he held her close against his chest. Her tiny head nestled into his shoulder, her long hair tickling his neck. And he loved every minute of it. She hadn't run to her blood grandmother or the grandmother of her heart or a mother figure. She'd run to him. To Uncle Eric.

Brushing a lock of hair behind her ear, he tipped his head back to look her in the eye. "Can you tell me what hurts?"

She held up her palms. The raw scrapes probably hurt him as much as they hurt her. Then she lifted a leg straight out, locking her skinned knees.

"Oh my. You got it good." He ran his hand along the untouched portion of skin. "We're going to have to get you cleaned up."

"No." She buried her head in his shoulder.

Hefting her higher up in his grasp, he tipped his head toward the house for Iris to follow. Behind him, Fiona, the General, Anne and her husband, and his father and grandfather trailed along. Everyone worried about Emily.

"Oh, what have we here?" Lucy came up to the little girl and clapping her hands lightly, reached out for Emily.

In complete contrast to the first day when Emily had so easily gone with Lucy, now she tightened the strangling hold around his neck.

"There's chocolate ice cream in the freezer," Lucy coaxed, and Emily's sobs slowed. "I bet we could get your uncle's permission for two scoops."

Emily lifted her head from his shoulder. He would have to remember to add chocolate ice cream to his bag of tricks once they left Hart Land.

"But," Lucy held up a finger, "we have to clean you up first."

Tiny fingers tightened around his neck, but Emily remained upright.

"How about if we let Lucy clean you up and then we all have ice cream?" He could probably figure out how to wash out a few scrapes, but until he got a better handle on the gentle end of dealing with a little girl, he'd just as soon Lucy did it.

Emily didn't move.

"I bet Lucy might even have some sprinkles for that ice cream."

"Rainbow?" Emily asked.

Eric didn't want to make any promises he, or Lucy, couldn't keep. He cast a sideways glance in the housekeeper's direction and spotted the slight head bob. "Rainbow," he confirmed.

Sliding down from his hold on her, as she'd done that first day, Emily extended her hand and followed Lucy's lead up to the house and into the kitchen.

Lips pressed tightly together, Anne Hughes sucked in a deep breath and blew it out slowly. "Uncle."

"Excuse me?" Eric asked.

"I cry uncle." Lifting her chin, she looked Eric in the eye. "I have been convinced that the children are happy here with you. And I have also been thoroughly reminded how much happier my son was with your sister, perhaps not in spite of her American ways, but because of them."

Eric nodded. He wasn't so sure about Adele and Richard, but he would take any concessions this prim and proper woman would give him.

"Mostly, that little display of unstaged affection confirms the children do indeed love you, and no matter how much I might want them closer to me, I can't possibly take away another person in their lives."

And for that, Eric was truly grateful.

Anne Hughes marched past him, pausing momentarily at his side. "But don't think I won't be watching." And just like that she was gone.

Walking past him, his grandfather smiled wide, and then his dad slowed his steps. "You're doing great. Really great."

Roberta paused at his side. "Adele knew this would happen."

"What?" His head whipped around.

"Why she picked you over my sister and me." Roberta shrugged. "Not that we're not wonderful aunt material, but she knew you were father material. Apparently, it has something to do with playing baseball, and video games, and not letting her drown."

Memories of Adele horning in on games with his friends came flooding back and made him smile. He and his friends always let her play and somehow he'd forgotten that despite all the swimming lessons, it was a vacation in Orlando where every afternoon he'd held her up in the pool while she practiced her kicks and breathing. She finally got it.

"She said you were the most patient and loving brother a girl could ever have. That never once did she feel she wasn't your equal or that anything she wanted was unattainable." A few silent seconds passed and Roberta nodded, taking a step back. "She was definitely right."

He stood perfectly still, watching Roberta, her sister, and the General's newly formed troops marching their way up to the house, then cast a glance down the hill to the Point. No matter how much faith his sister had in him, he had to wonder if things would have worked out so well had he never come here.

This place was perfection in many ways. Yes, the land was beautiful, yes, the family was great, but along with Emily and Gavin, one person in particular had become extremely important to him. He extended his hand and curled her fingers into his. "Walk with me a minute?"

Iris's eyes rounded, but without a word she nodded and fell into step beside him.

When was the last time simply holding a woman's hand in his made him feel like he could conquer the world? Maybe never.

"I can live anywhere with my job."

She nodded.

"Assuming I keep doing what I do." And he'd already decided whatever he does to earn a living, most of it would have to be done from home where the children were. "I could do this."

"Yes, you can," she agreed.

"I have a lot to learn still."

She smiled up at him. "Yes, but so does every parent."

Now he needed to consider carefully what he wanted—needed—to say next. "Have you given any more thought to what you're going to do when you go back to work?"

Her eyebrows lifted. "Some."

"Some?"

She nodded and he wished she'd given him more than a vague one word answer.

"Still contemplating a job that would keep you near the lake?"

"Yes." She kept her gaze ahead. "Cindy says Mrs. Ferguson at the elementary school is thinking of finally retiring."

"You're certified to teach too?" Nothing about the woman he loved surprised him any more.

"No, but I have a masters degree and that qualifies me to teach in this state."

Okay, he could work with that. Actually, his heart did a little two step. If she'd give him a chance, a real chance, he'd have plenty of time to talk her into helping him not with the kids, but with the rest of his life. "Here goes nothing." He pulled her around to face him and lifting his hand, rubbed the confused wrinkle from her forehead. "I would very much like to give us a chance. A real chance. Not a doofus guy needs a nanny, not a vacation time fling."

"Fling?" Her brows shot up but her eyes lit with amusement.

He rolled his eyes momentarily skyward. "If you're going to pick on me, I'll never get out what I want to say."

"Sorry." She smiled up at him, inching closer to him. "What do you want to say?"

The nearness of her breath against his chin sent his heart rate racing and all coherent thought slipped away.

"Eric," she coached.

"I want more for us. For all of us. And if you don't want to stay and work here at the lake, I want to go where you are." There. He'd said it.

"You do?" Was that hope he saw in her gaze?

He nodded. "Very much so."

"Why?"

"Why?" She wasn't going to make this easy on him, was she?

"That's the question on the table. Why?"

He sucked in another deep fortifying breath. Nothing ventured, nothing gained. "Because I'm in love with you."

It took a second for a slow, sweet smile to take over her face. She inched up on tippy toes and pressed sweet soft lips against his. "Guess it's pretty cool that I love you too."

"You do?"

She nodded.

"And you're not afraid of taking on the Queen of England?"

Her head swayed from side to side. "Not as long as we've got each other."

Pulling her into the fold of his arms, he let his hands fall to her waist. "Then you'd better strap yourself in, cause we're in for one helluva ride."

CHAPTER TWENTY-ONE -

EPILOGUE

Iris stood on the path from the car to her grandparents' home. Had anyone bet her even a few short weeks ago that she would have spent Easter morning surrounded by an army of young children hunting down colored eggs—and loved every minute of it—she'd have lost her savings.

"Yeah. I understand. Let me know." Eric hung up the phone and squeezed her hand.

"A job?" She knew that unlike a banker or a plumber, the type of work Eric did could take him away pretty far and possibly for pretty long.

"Maybe." Eric pulled her into the fold of his arms.

With the children around, they didn't do that nearly as often as either of them would have liked. The last few weeks had been heaven on earth. Maybe it was a little selfish of her, but she wasn't ready to let him go just yet.

"Gil's going to see if Kurt's up to it, but odds are pretty good it's going to have to be me. We can't chance anyone else. Not this time."

"I know." Iris let her head rest on his shoulder. The children and their grandparents would be back from town any minute and the rest of the family were waiting inside Hart House.

"There is a bright side. I won't lose a day traveling. This rig is in the Gulf. I'll be able to leave tonight and hit the problem first thing in the morning. That will at least save me a couple of days."

She was thankful for any small favor. "I'm more worried about Gavin. We've only now gotten him to not carry the cheetah around twenty-four seven. I hope this doesn't cause a setback."

"I know. Me too." He tucked his finger under her chin and nudged it upward. "Are you sure you're okay with this?"

She nodded and his lips descended on hers. A soft sweet touch that filled her heart to the brim. Life didn't get any better.

• • • •

"It is so wonderful having little children around again." Fiona Hart hung a blue and red handprint painting on the fridge with a couple of magnets.

"I have to admit," Lucy wiped her hands on her apron, "when their grandmother showed up at church with little Gavin in a suit and tie, and Emily in an outfit worthy of the Easter Parade on Fifth Avenue, I did not have high hopes for the church egg hunt."

Cindy snuck a spitzbuben from the nearby plate. "Didn't Emily just look adorable in the matching shoes and purse? I did so love patent leather as a kid."

"Can't say the same for your sisters." Lucy pulled the bacon wrapped asparagus from the oven. "Your mother finally gave up on Sunday dress shoes."

Cindy took a deep whiff. "Another thing I absolutely love is that asparagus. It's practically addicting."

Her grams chuckled. "Can't say I've ever heard anyone say that about asparagus before."

"Probably because no one makes it taste quite as good as Lucy."

"That's because it's made with love." The longtime housekeeper slid the trays onto the counter and reached for another. That woman had been loving them with food for decades. Cindy couldn't imagine not having Lucy around, despite her crazy antics.

"Well the hunt went much better than I expected." Iris came through the kitchen door with Eric at her side. "I thought for sure the Queen was going to say something about getting their Easter clothes dirty or shoes scuffed, but nope. Not a peep. The woman was all smiles and polite."

Eric curled Iris into his side and smiled down at her. "You do realize one of these days you're going to slip and call her the Queen to her face?"

"Nah." Iris flashed a playful smile. "I have years of experience suppressing my true feelings for stuffed shirts."

"Speaking of which," Grams looked up from ripping lettuce, "where are Mr. and Mrs. Hughes and the children? Supper is almost ready."

"They stayed a little longer so the kids could have ice cream with some of their friends." Eric showed no signs of letting Iris go. "Apparently grandparents are not subject to the no spoiling dinner rule."

"That's absolutely correct." Grams nodded.

Eric leaned against the wall and drew Iris more closely against him.

For the last few weeks Cindy had watched the bond between the two tighten. Because neither had full-time nine to five jobs, and Eric and the kids were still renting the Sycamore cabin, these two were the couple that Cindy saw more often than her sister or cousins. If she were honest with herself, as much as she loved her life, and she did, she couldn't help but feel a teeny tiny bit of an emptiness deep down when she looked at the sparkle in her cousin's eyes. Sometimes a warm cuddly kitten or tail-wagging puppy just didn't cut it.

"Okay," Heather came in from the dining room, "table's all set."

"And the drinks are on the buffet." Jake came to stand behind his fiancée, letting his hands rest on her shoulders.

Cindy didn't miss the gentle way his fingers kneaded into what were no doubt very tired muscles, or the grateful smile directed up at him. The silent communication made her both want to smile with shared joy and pout at the same time. Since pouting hadn't worked since she was two, she snatched another of her sister's cookies.

Clacking of doggy toenails clicked against the hardwood floors, announcing the General's arrival. "I can smell that roast all the way on the porch. I am officially starved."

"Good." Lucy slid the large pan out of the double oven. "As soon as Emily and Gavin arrive with their grandparents, you can carve."

Almost as if cued by the universe, the two children came scrambling in. As had been their ritual now since their uncle decided to make Lawford his new home base and the Hart House the heart of it, the two children split directions. Emily went first to Grams then the General, while Gavin did the opposite before the two barreled into their uncle. To any onlooker it appeared as if the main objective was to see if they could one day knock him over.

The huge grin that always took over Eric's face said he didn't mind one blessed bit.

"Easy," the British grandmother said from the doorway before her husband cleared his throat, shook his head, and then smiled at his wife's acquiescing sigh. Cindy supposed some day the poor woman would get used to her grandchildren's lack of British sensibilities. Maybe.

"Uncle Eric," Emily practically bounced in place, "Mr. McIntyre said that maybe next weekend we could take a ride on the firetruck."

Eric's gaze searched out Lily's soon to be husband.

"We've got a truck going in for annual servicing so it won't be on duty, so to speak," Cole confirmed.

"Do I get to go too?" Lily sidled up beside him. Balancing a plate of some tasty confection in one hand, she inched up on her tippy-toes and kissed Cole smack on the lips.

"Anytime," the man practically purred.

"I don't know about the rest of you," Cindy hopped off her stool, "but it's getting awfully warm in here."

At least Iris had the decency to blush before giving Eric a gentle peck on the cheek and following him and the others to the dining room. Pretty soon the double tables with extra chairs wouldn't be enough for the family if it continued to grow. Especially with the increasing tendency for all to descend on the lake, if not once a month, at least on key holidays.

"It is getting a bit crowded, isn't it?" Zinnia leaned in and whispered. "And is it me or do those two look ready to self combust?"

With all the romance abounding in Hart Land, Cindy actually had to follow Zinnia's glance to see which *two* her cousin was referring to. She had a point. With the children around, Iris and Eric seemed to rely more on furtive glances where the other newly joined couples freely indulged in stolen kisses, hand holding, and other low-keyed gestures of affection.

Abandoning their master, Sarge and Lady each took a spot beside one of the two children. Cindy suspected it had more to do with the amount of food that found its way to the floor more than a sense of guardianship, but she could be wrong.

The sound of a phone buzzing echoed in the crowded room. As folks meandered about pouring drinks and settling into seats, Eric glanced at his phone. The way his lips tightened into a flat line did not bode well.

"Kurt can't go?" Iris asked softly.

"No."

Iris nodded. Apparently, they both knew something the others did not.

"I'm afraid I'm going to have to skip the rest of the day," he announced to the table.

"Time to go back to work?" the General asked.

Eric nodded. "Hopefully I won't be gone more than a few days. Maybe a week."

The last words had Gavin's head snapping up. "You're going away?"

"Remember," Eric eased his way closer to his nephew, "we talked about this. I may have to go away from time to time because of my work."

The little boy's lower lip quivered. "Can I come with you?"

Eric drew the boy into a tight hug. "Not this time, champ. I need you to take care of Iris and Emily. I'm counting on you. Just like we talked about."

Cindy didn't know about anyone else in the room, but her heart was hurting for the little man.

"Our new family," the little boy muttered before crawling into Iris's lap. "I'll take care of you, Aunt Iris, don't you worry."

All eyes turned to Eric. No one missed the new use of 'aunt' before Iris's name.

"Well, we were going to make an official announcement after we had a chance to take care of a few more things, but since the cat is, what you might say, out of the bag..." He reached for Iris's hand and kissed the empty third finger of her left hand. "We'll be shopping for a ring as soon as I get back."

Cheers erupted and chairs skidded across the wood floors as family jumped to their feet. Hugs and congratulations abounded. The sound of a champagne cork popping put a stop to all the celebratory banter.

The General poured the first cup. "To the newest members of the Hart clan. Welcome Emily, Gavin and Eric."

"Thank you," he said to the world, but smiled down on his fiancée.

"And if you'll have us," the General offered another glass to the Queen who had surprisingly been the first to bolt around her seat and hug the newly engaged couple, "we'd be honored."

"The honor is all ours." The Queen smiled down at her grandchildren and the happy couple.

Whoever said fairytales didn't come true had never been around the Hart family. If Cindy were any happier for her cousin, she'd be the one to self combust. One by one the Hart granddaughters were finding their own Prince Charming in the most unexpected of places, and falling hard.

Yep. Cindy took a sip of the Champagne. Maybe some day one of those kittens or puppies would come with her own prince.

From Lily's Recipe Box

MANDEL BREAD
(similar to biscotti)

What you'll need:

1 stick salted butter
¾ cup sugar
1 teaspoon vanilla
2 eggs
2 cups flour
1 teaspoon baking powder
1 cup chocolate chips
Cinnamon
Dash of almond extract (optional – Lily uses a capful of extract which is about ¼ teaspoon)
½ c sliced almonds (optional)

Instructions:

Preheat oven to 350 degrees.
Cream butter & sugar.
Add eggs and extract.
Mix well.
Add flour, baking powder.
Mix in chocolate chips and almonds.
Dough will be sticky.
Dust cookie sheet and your fingers with flour and form dough into 3 logs.
Sprinkle top of logs with cinnamon.
Bake 35 minutes or until golden brown.
Cool about 15 minutes.

Cut each log into slices on the diagonal and place the slices on the cookie sheet.
Bake again an additional 15-17 minutes until desired crispness.

Note: These are yummy with morning coffee.

Excerpt from HYACINTH

Find a nice quiet place, he'd said. Leave the modern world behind, he'd said. You'll get more work done, he'd said. I know the perfect place, retired Marine Colonel Francis Stewart had insisted. At least Alan Stewart's grandfather had been right about something; Lake Lawford was one of the most beautiful and peaceful places he'd ever been.

Too bad it wasn't doing a dang thing for his productivity. At this point, Alan was so far behind he could see his own shadow. Not even the dummy in the middle of the room was helping. Weaving his fingers together, he stretched his arms, the cracking of knuckles filling the air. Now if only the sound of fingers tapping on the keyboard could do the same. Staring at the screen he shook his head. Why was this suddenly so difficult? For almost a month he'd been holed up in this cabin searching for his mojo. Actually, twenty-nine days, fourteen hours and, he glanced at the lower corner of the laptop screen, twenty minutes, but who was counting.

Lifting his hands to his arms to rub away a chill, he turned his attention to the fireplace and the intricate structure of logs and kindling waiting to be lit. Not something folks raised in the south learned to build. For the last month temperatures had fooled everyone into believing summer had come early to New England. Not once had it occurred to him to light a fire; he'd done little more than admire the pile of logs. Until now. Today he wondered if Mother Nature was off her meds again.

Since nothing else was working, pushing his seat away from the small desk, Alan crossed the room, shook his head at poor Harvey taped to the chair, and hunched down in front of the old stone fireplace. Somewhere there had to be matches. It took a few seconds to realize that the lovely foot-long hand-painted box to the right of the carved mantle held the matches he needed. It took another moment to discover that the underside of the box was the strike plate. Maybe he'd buy the cabin owner a lighter gun. Not as pretty, but much more practical. Any man who had ever lit a barbecue knew that.

Only two attempts and gloating in his caveman success, he held the lit stick to the crumpled newspaper stuffed under the logs with the kindling. It only took a moment for the paper to catch. Who said back to nature wasn't easy? Another second and the flames shot up like an erupting volcano. The surprise of it all knocked Alan back on his haunches. Well, flat on his backside, but who was he going to tell?

Shoving upright, he returned to his makeshift desk. Maybe once he warmed up he could get some work done. The snap and crackle of the newly lit fire was like a mesmerizing melody. Already the heat filled the room and warmed his bones. Rubbing his hands together, he laid his fingers on the keys eager to feel the words come to life.

Unfortunately, the only thing coming to life was the smoke in the chimney. Like tendrils in a horror flick, gray waves filled the room. Now what? Shoving his chair back he jumped to his feet, bolted across the room, and stared at the smoking fireplace. He should've just raised the thermostat. Vaguely remembering having seen a fire extinguisher under the kitchen sink, he pivoted in that direction and from the corner of his eye spotted a large framed lettering propped prominently on the mantle. *OPEN the flu before starting a fire.* Of course. But who in heaven's name wants to stick their arm up a raging fire to open a flu.

To the right a stand of iron utensils held one potentially helpful piece. Suddenly the crook end of a poker made sense. It had nothing to do with pushing and moving logs, it was all about idiots like him who forgot to open the flue. By the time he located the metal lever and pushed it to the opposite position, he might as well have been standing by San Francisco Bay on a foggy fall day. Even though the fireplace now sucked smoke up the chimney, it did nothing for the blanket of smoke hovering in the tiny cabin's living room.

Freezing cold or not, he had no choice. He opened one window, then the other, and waving his arms madly, opened the front door wide. All he needed now was for some neighbor to call Hart House and report he'd set the place on fire. Grabbing his notebook and the nearby magazine, he did his best to dissipate the cloud of smoke. So focused skyward on his efforts, he almost missed the big tan streak dashing from the porch through the front door and past his ankles until it almost knocked him over and darted down the narrow hall. Quickly, panic licked at his racing heart. What the heck was that? He'd spent more than one afternoon sitting on the front porch and had yet to see anything approach the cabin. He'd spotted a couple of deer up the hillside in the trees, but none of them had been young.

Though now that he thought about it, wasn't spring the time for all new critters. Could it have been a baby deer that flew past him? Wouldn't he look silly calling animal control over a baby fawn. Shaking his head, he walked down the hall, hesitating a moment by the kitchen to grab a broom. Just in case. The only open door led to his room. A space too small for anything to hide. Actually, he expected to find the scared and nervous fawn huddling in a corner. When the room looked completely untouched, that meant one thing—whatever had come inside was under the bed.

Sucking in a deep breath, he reminded himself this was not a television show or a horror flick, or even a Stephen King novel. His imagination was probably worse than whatever was actually hiding under the bed. Not standing too close, just in case, he got down on all fours and carefully tilted his head into the dark space. His first concern should have been the rumbling growl that vibrated under the low mattress. He was pretty sure fawns didn't growl. Glowing green eyes met his. He had absolutely no idea what animal had green eyes and growled, but by the time his brain registered the snarling teeth, he was up and out of that room faster than a speeding bullet. Imagination be damned.

At least he was proud of himself for two things. One, not getting mauled to death. Two, having kept his wits about him enough to close the door behind him. Searching for his phone somewhere on the table, his mind ran through a list of the most likely angry critters that could roam the nearby woods. Mountain lion—okay, maybe a bobcat—kept jumping to the top of the list. Neither of which he could see Fiona Hart or George the handyman grappling with. Like it or not, he needed serious help.

• • • • •

"Well, top of the morning to you." Katie O'Leary smiled up at Cindy as she came around the corner, arms laden with several loaves of the shop owner's famed Irish soda bread.

"And the rest of the day to you," Cindy answered. As kids, the traditional Irish response had been a joke. As an adult, she savored any opportunity to be transported to a kinder, gentler place and time. Any chance to spend time with Katie O'Leary did that. Even though she'd been born on this mountain, raised by her Irish grandmother, she had enough of the Emerald Isle in her to be a breath of fresh air to anyone who crossed her path.

"Looks like you're feeding an army."

Cindy laughed. "Not quite. Lucy asked me to come by and pick up a few things. The General has had a hankering for her corned beef, and since the grocery store had a big sale on point end corned beef, Lucy saw no reason not to accommodate him."

"And a good job of accommodating the entire family she does."

"Absolutely." Cindy could not argue. Lucy was technically her grandparents' housekeeper and cook, but as far as the grandchildren were concerned, she was family. There wasn't a thing any of them would not do for Lucy, and she was pretty sure there was not a thing Lucy wouldn't do for them. Though most of them agreed, they wished that Lucy would stick to cooking and cleaning, and bypass the Dolly Levi matchmaking.

"Has Lucy had any luck in getting that young hermit out of his cabin?"

Cindy shook her head. "The man doesn't open his door for anyone. The few times he's asked for room service, he's told Lucy to have George leave it on the porch."

"I'm wondering if maybe the man has an embarrassment to hide. You know, a nose like Cyrano de Bergerac, or a chin like the Wicked Witch of the West."

"Or a mask like the Phantom of the Opera?" Cindy smiled.

Katie shook her head. "Now I won't be making anything that dramatic. But the man must have a strong reason to keep to himself for this long. He hasn't come into town for anything. This time, I'm thinking Lucy may be right. It may be time for some of us folks to make an extra effort to bring the man out of his shell."

"Out of his shell?" Cindy narrowed her gaze, interpreting the simple comment and hoping it did not mean Lucy was up to her old tricks.

"Now don't you look at me like that. I'm not the one who wants your sister Poppy to start making the deliveries to the cabin instead of George."

She knew it. Would Lucy never learn. Heaving out a sigh, Cindy supposed she should be grateful that Lucy wasn't planning on locking her sister in the cabin with the man, or poisoning his food so that someone would have to stay and care for him. Or would she?

"And what has your face suddenly looking like you sucked on a lemon?" Katie asked, placing the loaves of fresh bread in a cardboard box along with some of the other items Cindy had picked up.

"Nothing." She shook her head. Even Lucy wouldn't stoop that low. After all, as much as folks teased her about setting the house on fire, she didn't actually set it on fire. Cindy shook her head again. Now she was just being silly. Placing a few more items in a second box, she looked up at her smiling shopkeeper. "I think this is it."

"Excellent. Let me help you to the car." Katie came around the counter.

Cindy waved her off. Placing one box on her hip, she reached for the other box with her free arm. "They don't weigh much. I can do this."

"Of course you can. And I suppose you're going to open the car doors with your teeth?" Chuckling at her, Katie grabbed the second box and started for the exit.

"Thank you." Cindy walked out the door that Katie held, her gaze spotting a big red fox darting across the road at the same time a car sped out of the neighboring road. Her heart lurched in her throat. Yakking with the person in the passenger's seat, the driver obviously did not see the animal in its path.

"What is it dear?" Katie came to stand beside her, quickly seeing the same thing she did. "Oh, dear."

As sure as her name was Hyacinth Nelson, DVM, the car knocked the poor animal halfway across the road and kept going. "Damn it." Practically dropping the box, she hurried to the curb, waiting to see if the fox would shake it off and get up or if he was more seriously injured. When the animal remained lifeless in the middle of the road, she shook her head.

Katie had no doubt been waiting for the same thing. "I've got some blankets in the back. I'll go get them. If he's not out cold, you're going to need something to help trap him."

Nodding, Cindy ran to her vehicle and pulled out her veterinary bag. This was another reason why the mountain desperately needed its own wildlife center for rescue and rehabilitation. Her small clinic was full up and too understaffed to keep a full-time eye on an injured fox. Hurrying across the road and hoping the little guy would just wake up and run off before she got there, a small pup waddled out from under a bush to stand beside his hurt parent. *Double blast.* Since fathers and mothers both parented their pups, she couldn't see from this distance if the mother or father had been hit, but if the snarling little one had his way, she wasn't going to get close enough to find out.

Heels clacking rapidly on the pavement, Katie appeared beside her, holding a pet carrier in one hand and blankets in the other. "Oh my. Where there is one, there has to be more."

"That's exactly what I was thinking." Cindy looked around for signs of more pups, but so far this was the only one. "Now all I have to do is get close enough without having that little one snap at me."

Katie nodded. "I'll take care of that."

Shooting her arm out to stop the woman from hurrying any closer to the injured animal, Cindy shook her head. "The last thing I need on top of an injured wild animal is to have you hurt as well."

"Nonsense, that little fella's teeth won't do any damage."

Cindy tried really hard not to roll her eyes. When it came to any wild animal, even a fox, it wasn't just the bite she worried about. Any disease the animals carried, including rabies, could pose a much bigger problem. "Let me see how close I can get."

"Lass," Katie touched her arm, "I know you have a way with the animals, but there are two of them and two of us. Let's do this together."

As much as Cindy did not want to risk Katie getting hurt, she knew the woman was right. She also knew Katie had a way with people and animals alike. She just hoped this was one of those times when Katie's special way would work its magic.

Slowly inching toward the two animals and hoping no clueless driver would come barreling up the road, Cindy crouched, speaking softly to the still snarling and snapping pup beside its dead or unconscious parent. "Easy fella. No one is going to hurt you."

Stepping around her, Katie softly moved ahead, smiling at the pup. She didn't say a word. She merely sat down just outside of snapping distance, opened the blanket on her lap, made a ticking sound with her throat, and much to Cindy's surprise, the little guy stopped snarling.

"Okay. Maybe I need to hire you to work at the clinic." Heaven knew, Cindy and her techs had been snapped, bitten, and scratched by more four legged creatures than she cared to admit.

Not wanting to interrupt the connection between Katie and the pup now tilting its head and studying the shopkeeper, Cindy debated how close she dared get to the injured fox. In the next second, the decision was made for her. The furry guy made up his mind as well. Without hesitation, he walked straight into Katie's lap and curled into a fluffy ball.

"No maybe." Cindy chuckled. "I definitely need to hire you for the clinic."

Wrapping the ends of the small blanket around the baby fox, Katie ignored the compliment. "Now you can check on the mama."

Turning her head, Cindy got a better look at the injured fox. She was indeed the mama. And thankfully, she was still alive. Now all she had to do was get the girl to the clinic and pray she could fix her up in time to reunite her with the rest of the pups.

Available at your favorite bookseller.

MEET CHRIS

USA TODAY Bestselling Author of more than a dozen contemporary novels, including the award-winning *Champagne Sisterhood*, Chris Keniston lives in suburban Dallas with her husband, two human children, and two canine children. Though she loves her puppies equally, she admits being especially attached to her German Shepherd rescue. After all, even dogs deserve a happily ever after.

More on Chris and her books can be found at
www.chriskeniston.com

Follow Chris on Facebook at ChrisKenistonAuthor
or on Twitter @ckenistonauthor

Questions? Comments?
I would love to hear from you.
You can reach me at chris@chriskeniston.com

www.ingramcontent.com/pod-product-compliance
Lightning Source LLC
Chambersburg PA
CBHW030639190726
48286CB00008B/2582